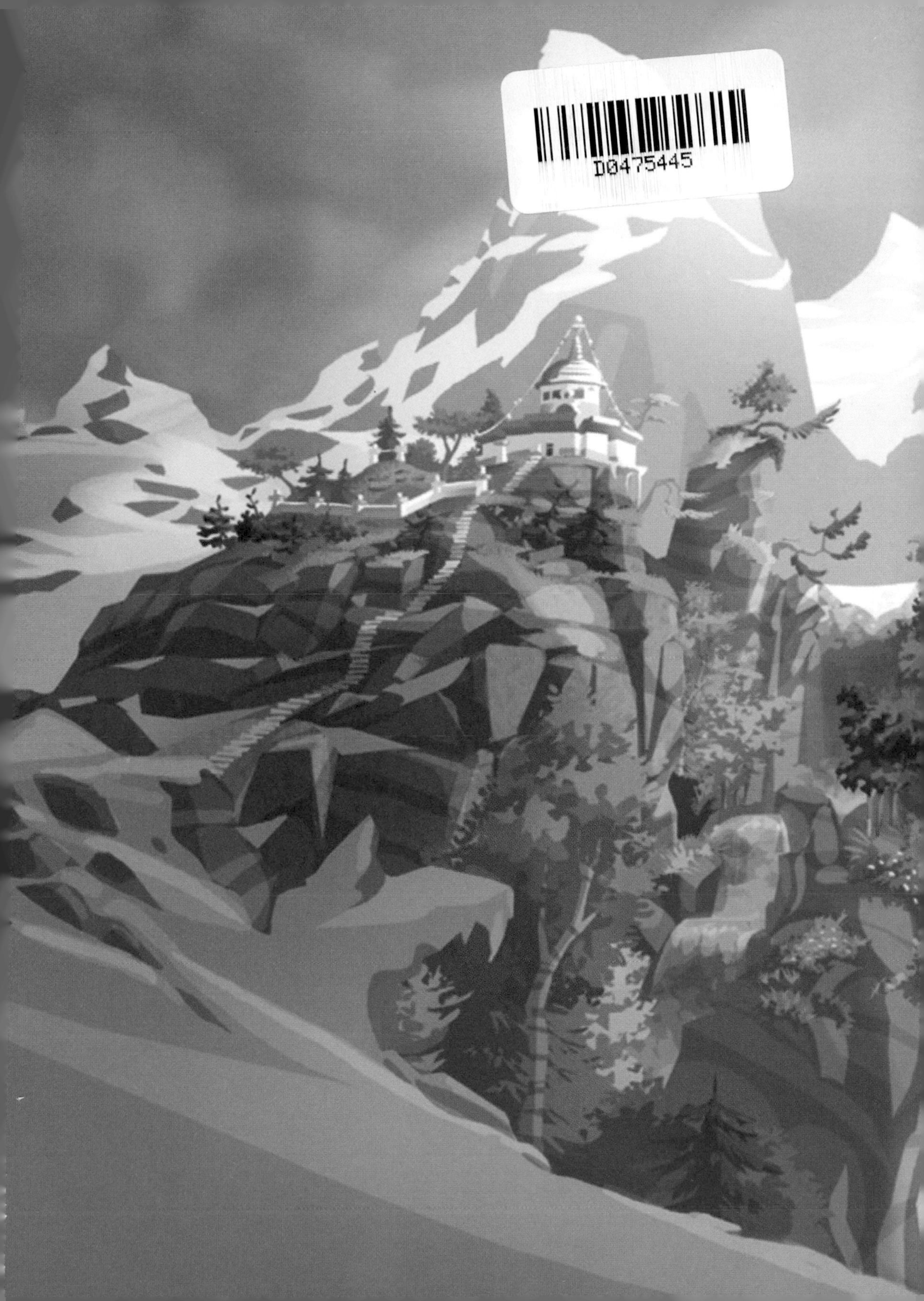

Geronimo Stilton™ Reporter

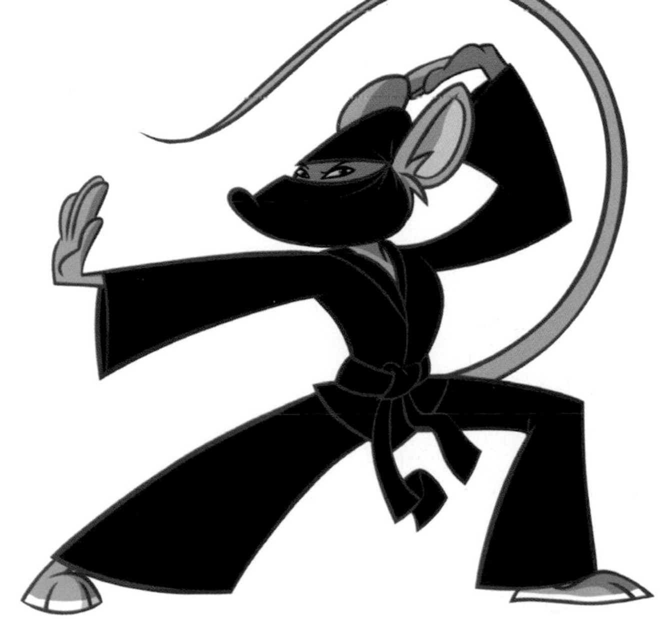

PAPERCUTZ™

Geronimo Stilton

GRAPHIC NOVELS AVAILABLE FROM PAPERCUTZ

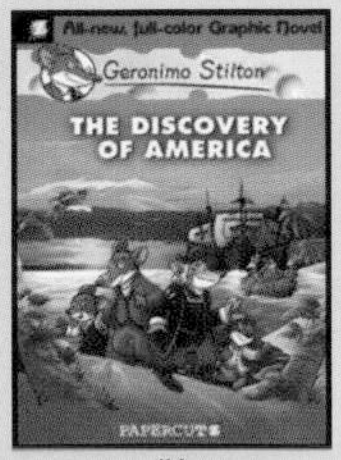
Geronimo Stilton
THE DISCOVERY OF AMERICA
#1 "The Discovery of America"

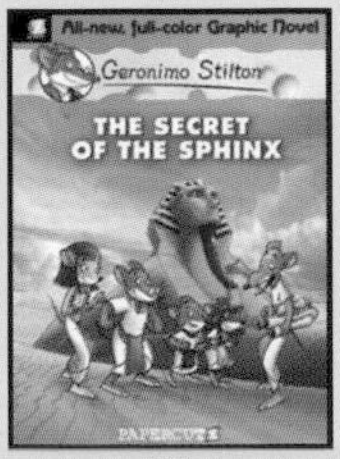
Geronimo Stilton
THE SECRET OF THE SPHINX
#2 "The Secret of the Sphinx"

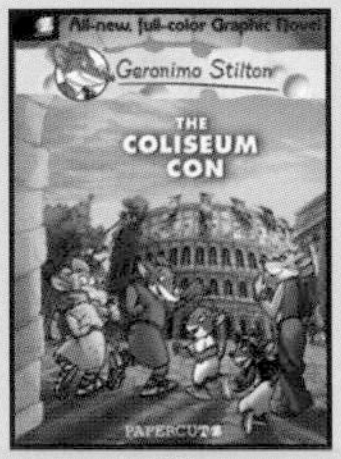
Geronimo Stilton
THE COLISEUM CON
#3 "The Coliseum Con"

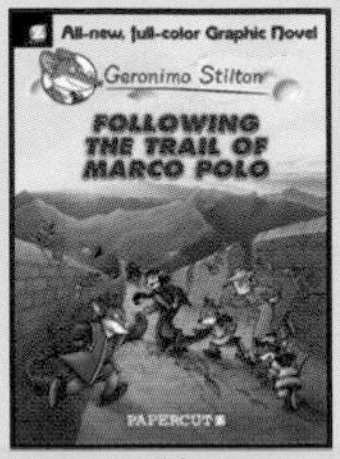
Geronimo Stilton
FOLLOWING THE TRAIL OF MARCO POLO
#4 "Following the Trail of Marco Polo"

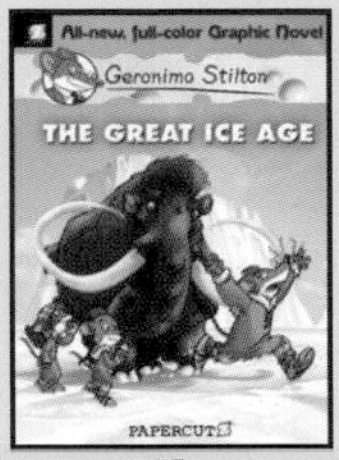
Geronimo Stilton
THE GREAT ICE AGE
#5 "The Great Ice Age"

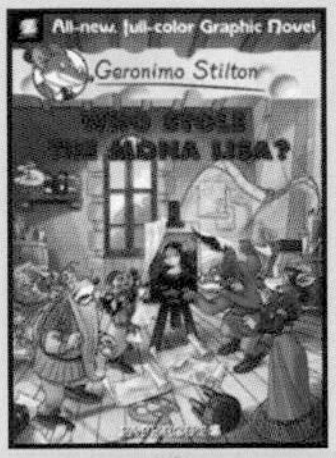
Geronimo Stilton
#6 "Who Stole The Mona Lisa?"

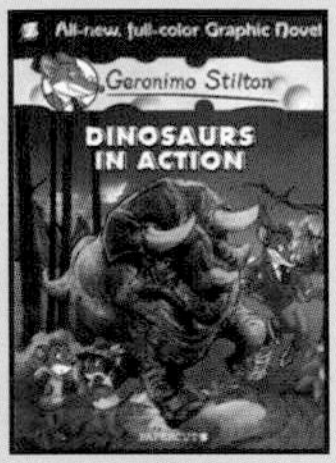
Geronimo Stilton
DINOSAURS IN ACTION
#7 "Dinosaurs in Action"

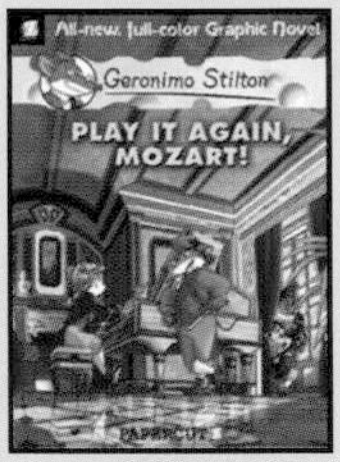
Geronimo Stilton
PLAY IT AGAIN, MOZART!
#8 "Play It Again, Mozart!"

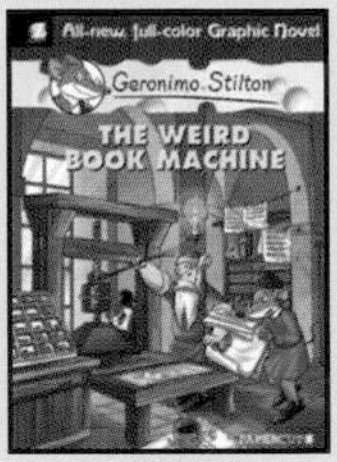
Geronimo Stilton
THE WEIRD BOOK MACHINE
#9 "The Weird Book Machine"

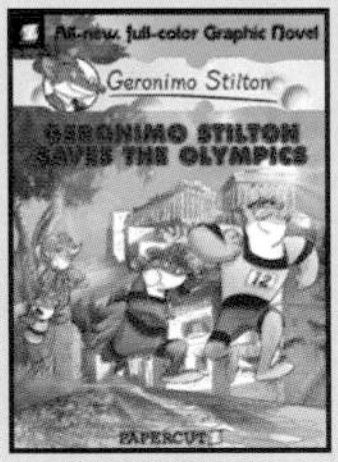
Geronimo Stilton
GERONIMO STILTON SAVES THE OLYMPICS
#10 "Geronimo Stilton Saves the Olympics"

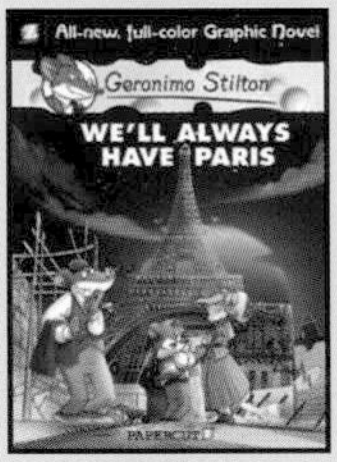
Geronimo Stilton
WE'LL ALWAYS HAVE PARIS
#11 "We'll Always Have Paris"

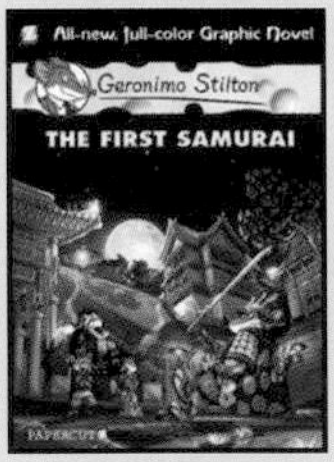
Geronimo Stilton
THE FIRST SAMURAI
#12 "The First Samurai"

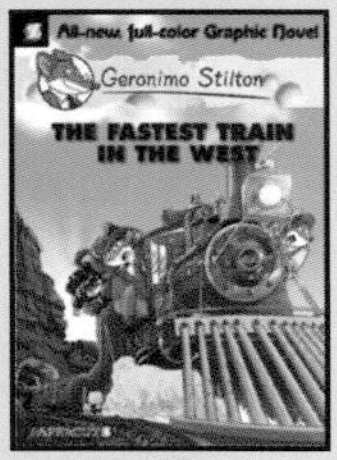
Geronimo Stilton
THE FASTEST TRAIN IN THE WEST
#13 "The Fastest Train in the West"

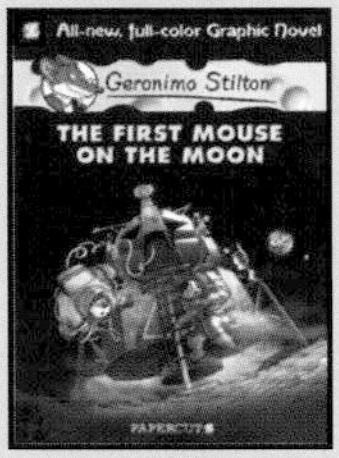
Geronimo Stilton
THE FIRST MOUSE ON THE MOON
#14 "The First Mouse on the Moon"

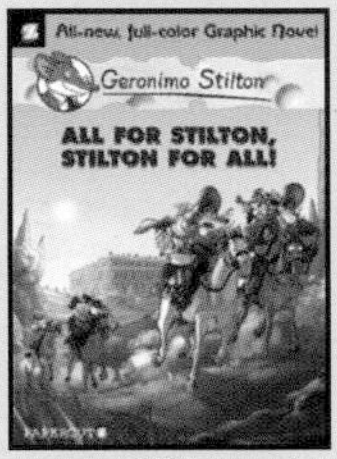
Geronimo Stilton
ALL FOR STILTON, STILTON FOR ALL!
#15 "All for Stilton, Stilton for All!"

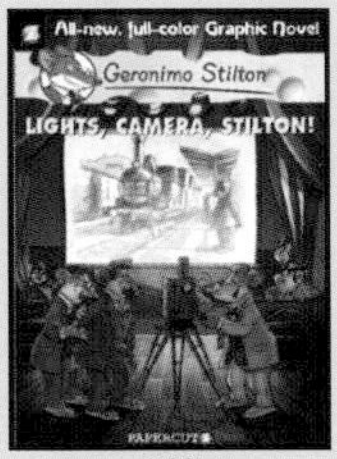
Geronimo Stilton
LIGHTS, CAMERA, STILTON!
#16 "Lights, Camera, Stilton!"

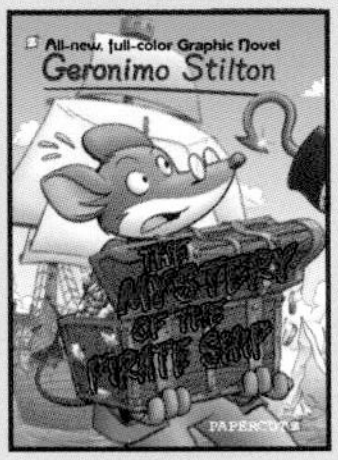
Geronimo Stilton
#17 "The Mystery of the Pirate Ship"

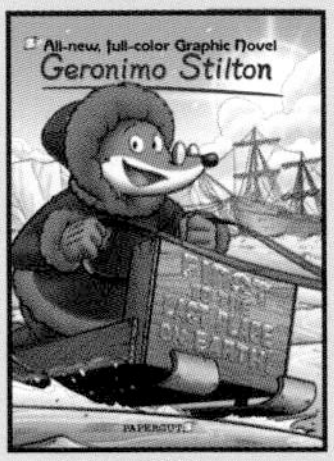
Geronimo Stilton
#18 "First to the Last Place on Earth"

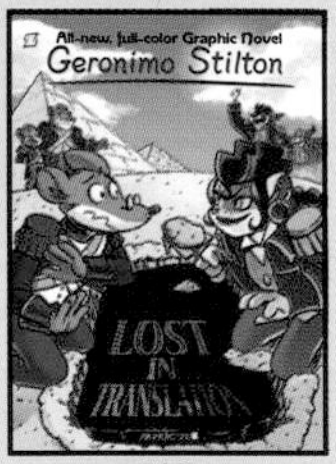
Geronimo Stilton
LOST IN TRANSLATION
#19 "Lost in Translation"

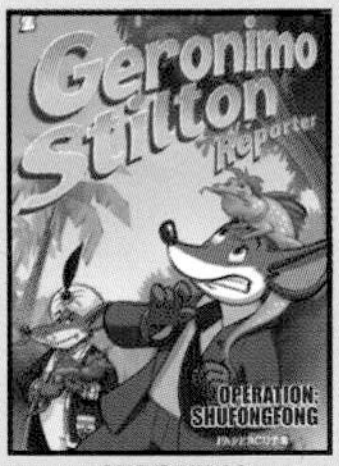
Geronimo Stilton
Reporter
OPERATION: SHUFONGFONG
GERONIMO STILTON REPORTER #1 "Operation ShuFongfong"

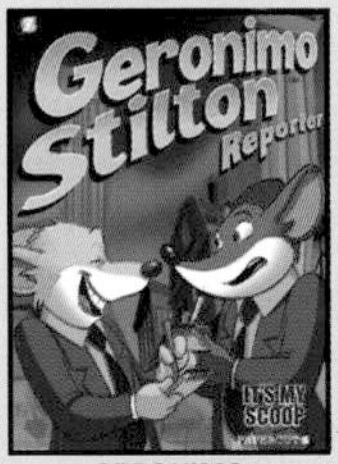
Geronimo Stilton
Reporter
IT'S MY SCOOP
GERONIMO STILTON REPORTER #2 "It's My Scoop"

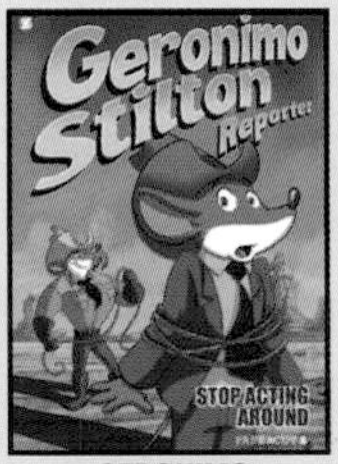
Geronimo Stilton
Reporter
STOP ACTING AROUND
GERONIMO STILTON REPORTER #3 "Stop Acting Around"

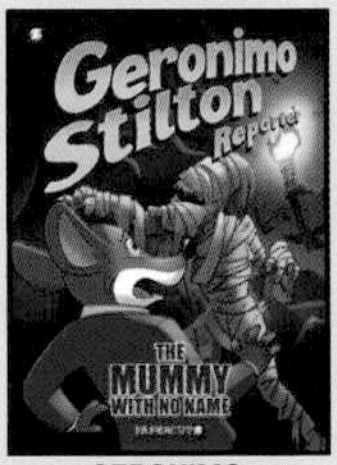
Geronimo Stilton
Reporter
THE MUMMY WITH NO NAME
GERONIMO STILTON REPORTER #4 "The Mummy with No Name"

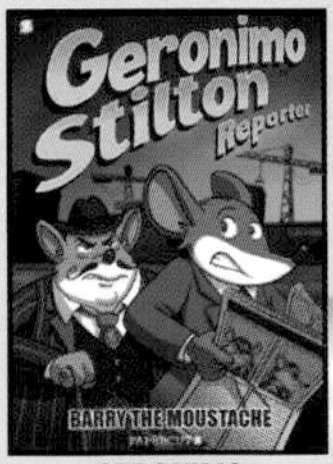
Geronimo Stilton
Reporter
BARRY THE MOUSTACHE
GERONIMO STILTON REPORTER #5 "Barry the Moustache"

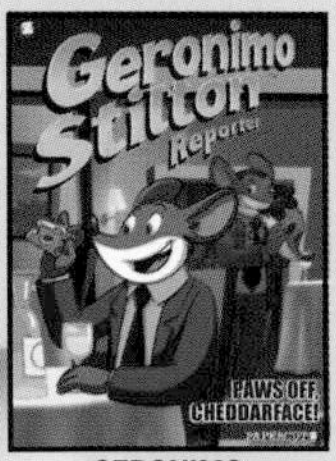
Geronimo Stilton
Reporter
PAWS OFF, CHEDDARFACE!
GERONIMO STILTON REPORTER #6 "Paws Off, Cheddarface!"

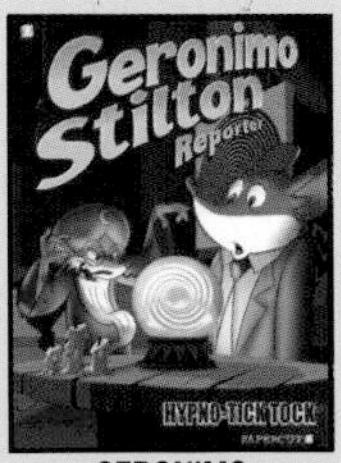
Geronimo Stilton
Reporter
HYPNO-TICK TOCK
GERONIMO STILTON REPORTER #8 "Hypno-Tick Tock"

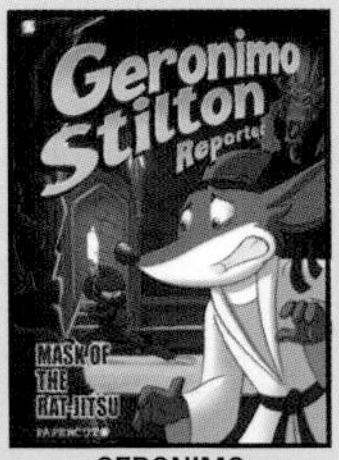
Geronimo Stilton
Reporter
MASK OF THE RAT-JITSU
GERONIMO STILTON REPORTER #9 "Mask of the Rat-Jitsu"

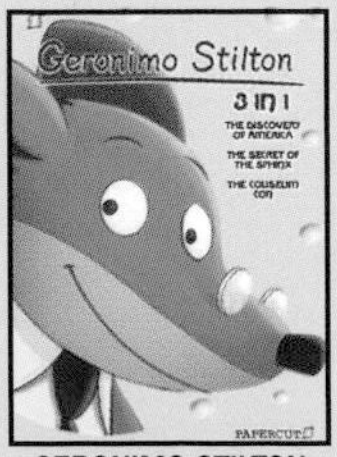
Geronimo Stilton
3 in 1
GERONIMO STILTON 3 in 1 #1

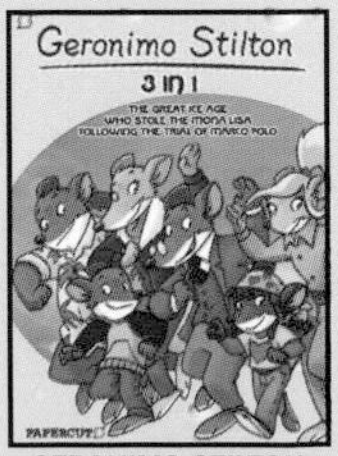
Geronimo Stilton
3 in 1
GERONIMO STILTON 3 in 1 #2

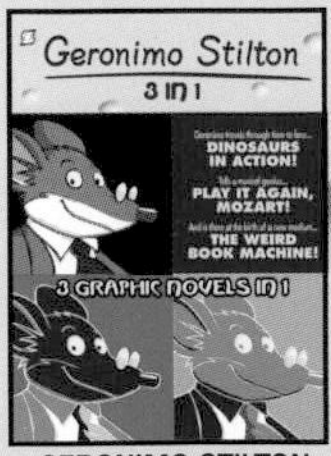
Geronimo Stilton
3 in 1
3 GRAPHIC NOVELS IN 1
GERONIMO STILTON 3 in 1 #3

...ALSO AVAILABLE WHEREVER E-BOOKS ARE SOLD!

See more at papercutz.com

Geronimo Stilton™ Reporter

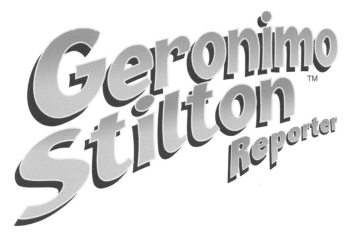

#9 MASK OF THE RAT-JITSU

By Geronimo Stilton

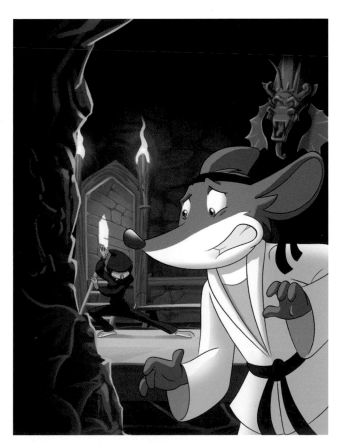

PAPERCUTZ™
NEW YORK

Geronimo Stilton Reporter

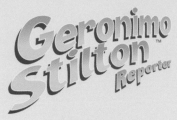

MASK OF THE RAT-JITSU

Text by Geronimo Stilton
Cover by ALESSANDRO MUSCILLO (artist) and CHRISTIAN ALIPRANDI (colorist)
Editorial supervision by ALESSANDRA BERELLO (Atlantyca S.p.A.)
Editing by ANITA DENTI (Atlantyca S.p.A.)
Script by DARIO SICCHIO
Art by ALESSANDRO MUSCILLO
Color by CHRISTIAN ALIPRANDI
Original Lettering by MARIA LETIZIA MIRABELLA

Special thanks to CARMEN CASTILLO

Based on an original idea by ELISABETTA DAMI.
Based on episode 9 of the Geronimo Stilton animated series "*Il Gran Torneo dei Guerrieri Topitsu,*" ["Mask of the Rat-Jitsu"]
written by DIANE MOREL, storyboard by JEAN TEXIER
Preview based on episode 10 of the Geronimo Stilton animated series "*Il tesoro di Baffonero,*" ["Blackrat's Treasure"]
written by DIANE MOREL, storyboard by RICCARDO AUDISIO
www.geronimostilton.com

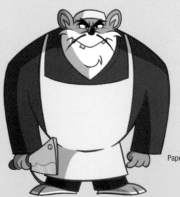

JAYJAY JACKSON — Production
WILSON RAMOS JR. — Lettering
JEFF WHITMAN — Managing Editor
LILY LU — Editorial Intern
JIM SALICRUP
Editor-in-Chief

ISBN: 978-1-5458-0729-3

Printed in India
November 2021

Papercutz books may be purchased for business or promotional use.
For information on bulk purchases please contact
Macmillan Corporate and Premium Sales
Department at (800) 221-7945x5442.

Distributed by Macmillan
First Printing

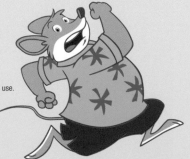

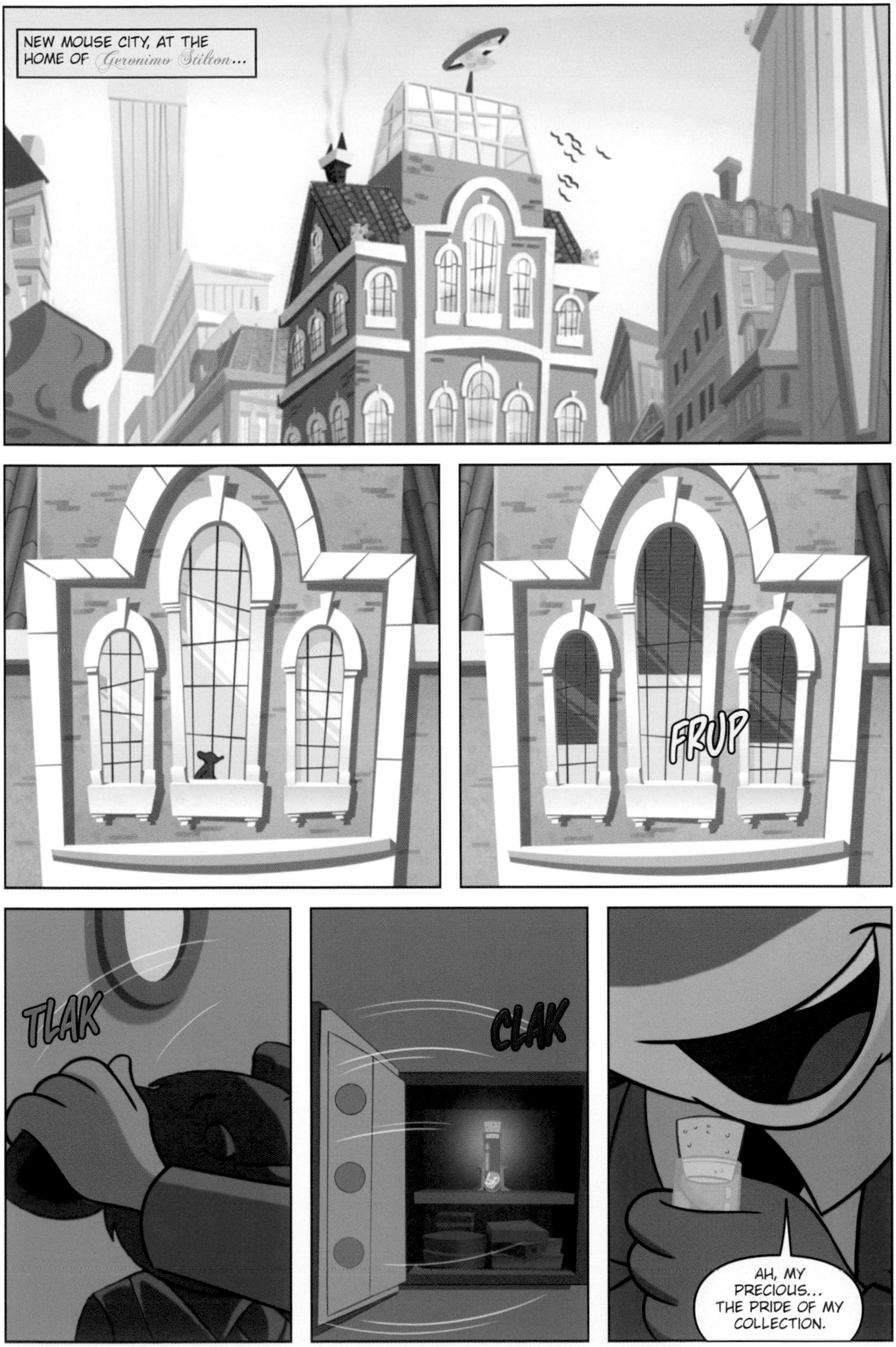
NEW MOUSE CITY, AT THE HOME OF Geronimo Stilton...
FRUP
TLAK
CLAK
AH, MY PRECIOUS... THE PRIDE OF MY COLLECTION.

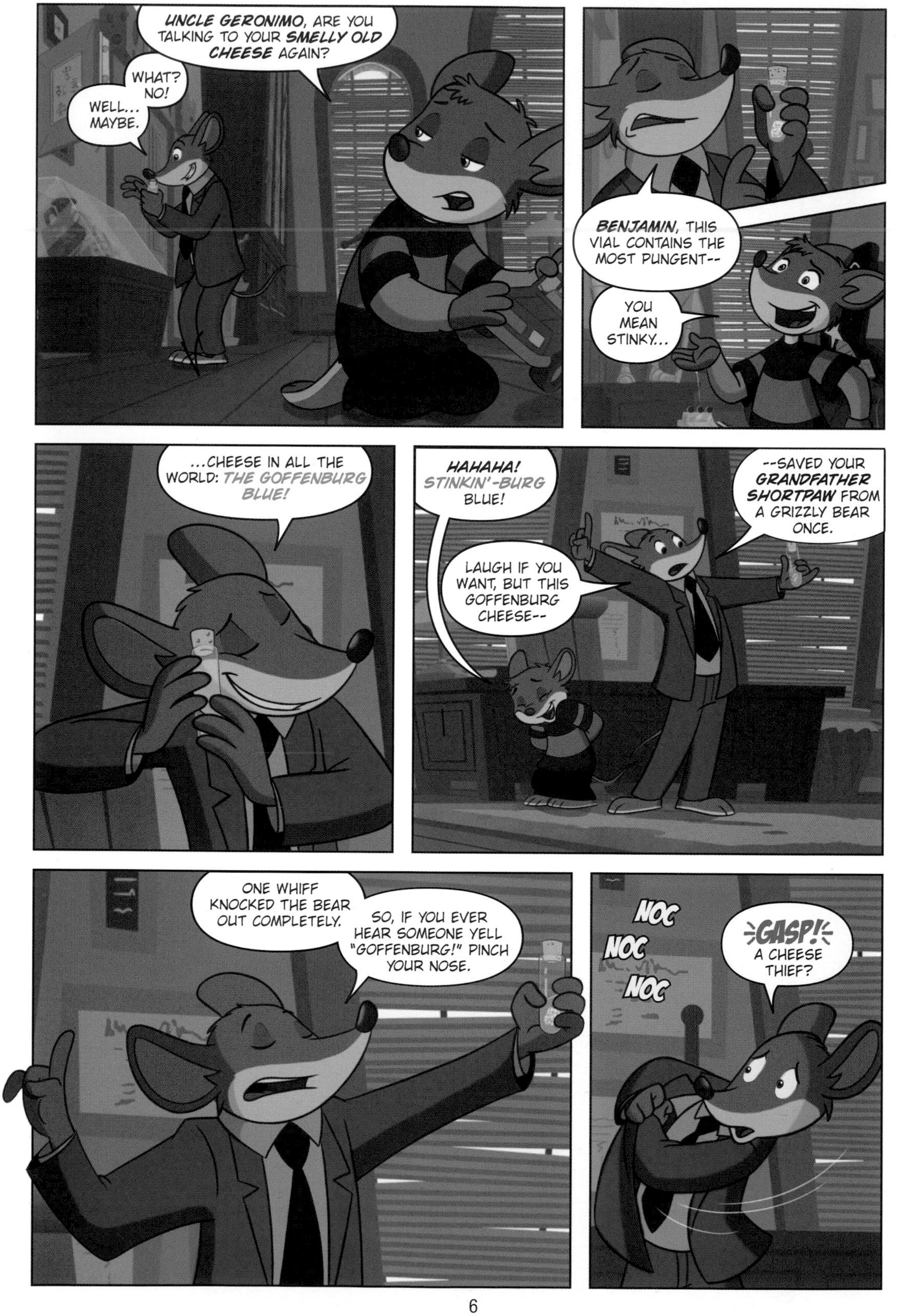
UNCLE GERONIMO, ARE YOU TALKING TO YOUR SMELLY OLD CHEESE AGAIN?
WHAT? NO!
WELL... MAYBE.
BENJAMIN, THIS VIAL CONTAINS THE MOST PUNGENT--
YOU MEAN STINKY...
...CHEESE IN ALL THE WORLD: THE GOFFENBURG BLUE!
HAHAHA! STINKIN'-BURG BLUE!
LAUGH IF YOU WANT, BUT THIS GOFFENBURG CHEESE--
--SAVED YOUR GRANDFATHER SHORTPAW FROM A GRIZZLY BEAR ONCE.
ONE WHIFF KNOCKED THE BEAR OUT COMPLETELY.
SO, IF YOU EVER HEAR SOMEONE YELL "GOFFENBURG!" PINCH YOUR NOSE.
NOC
NOC
NOC
GASP! A CHEESE THIEF?

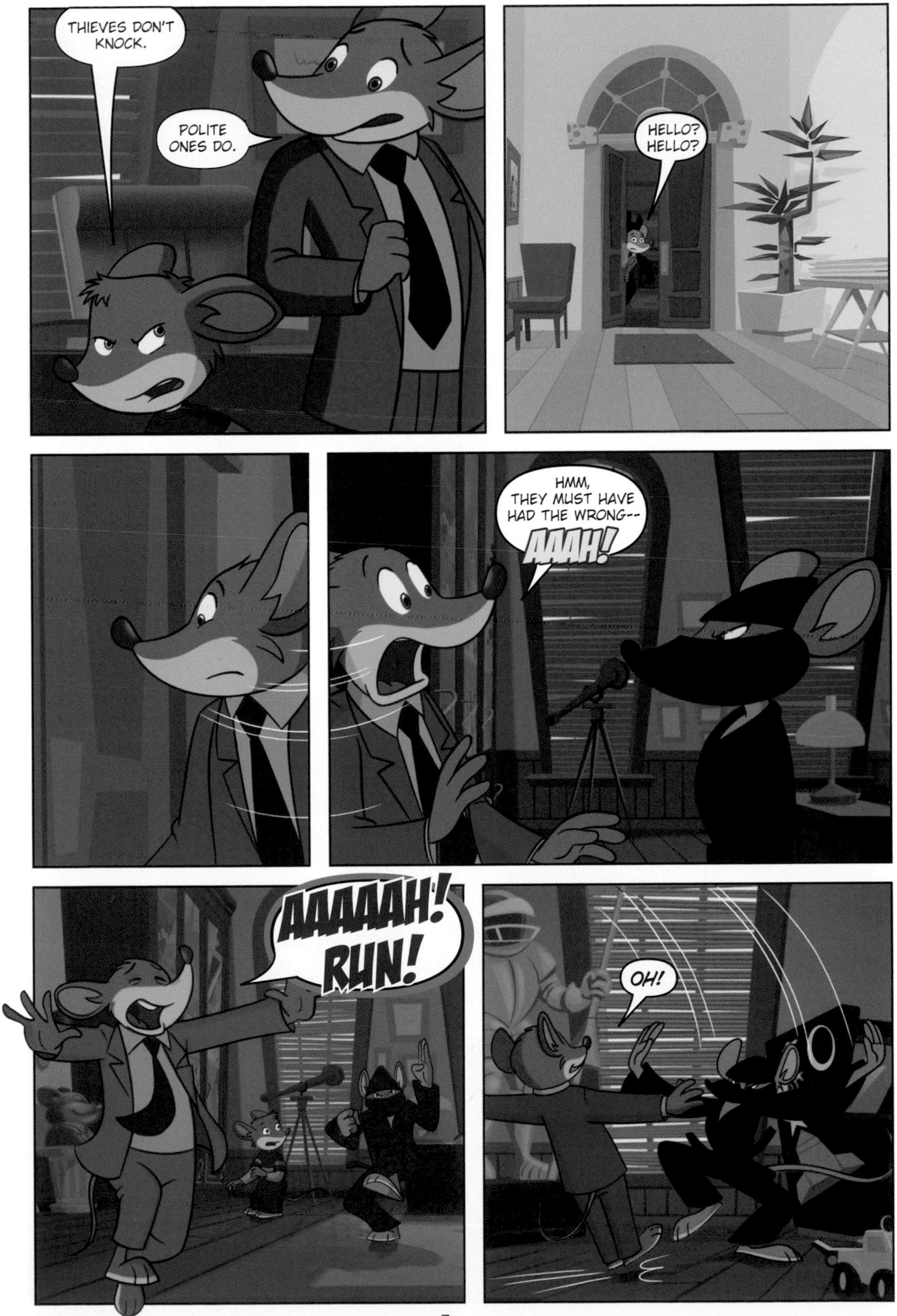

THIEVES DON'T KNOCK.
POLITE ONES DO.
HELLO? HELLO?
HMM, THEY MUST HAVE HAD THE WRONG--
AAAH!
AAAAAH! RUN!
OH!

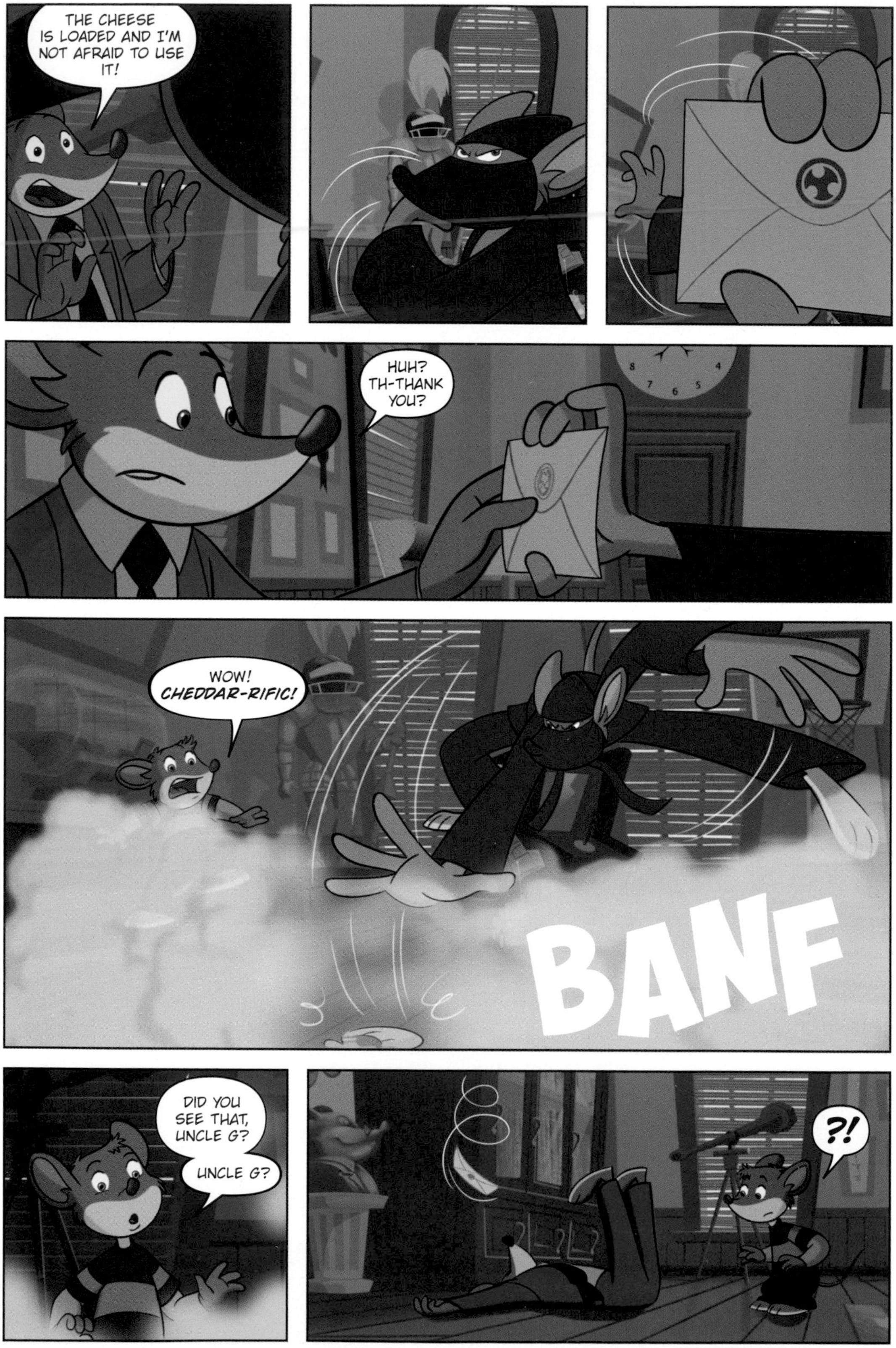
THE CHEESE IS LOADED AND I'M NOT AFRAID TO USE IT!
HUH? TH-THANK YOU?
WOW! CHEDDAR-RIFIC!
BANF
DID YOU SEE THAT, UNCLE G?
UNCLE G?
?!

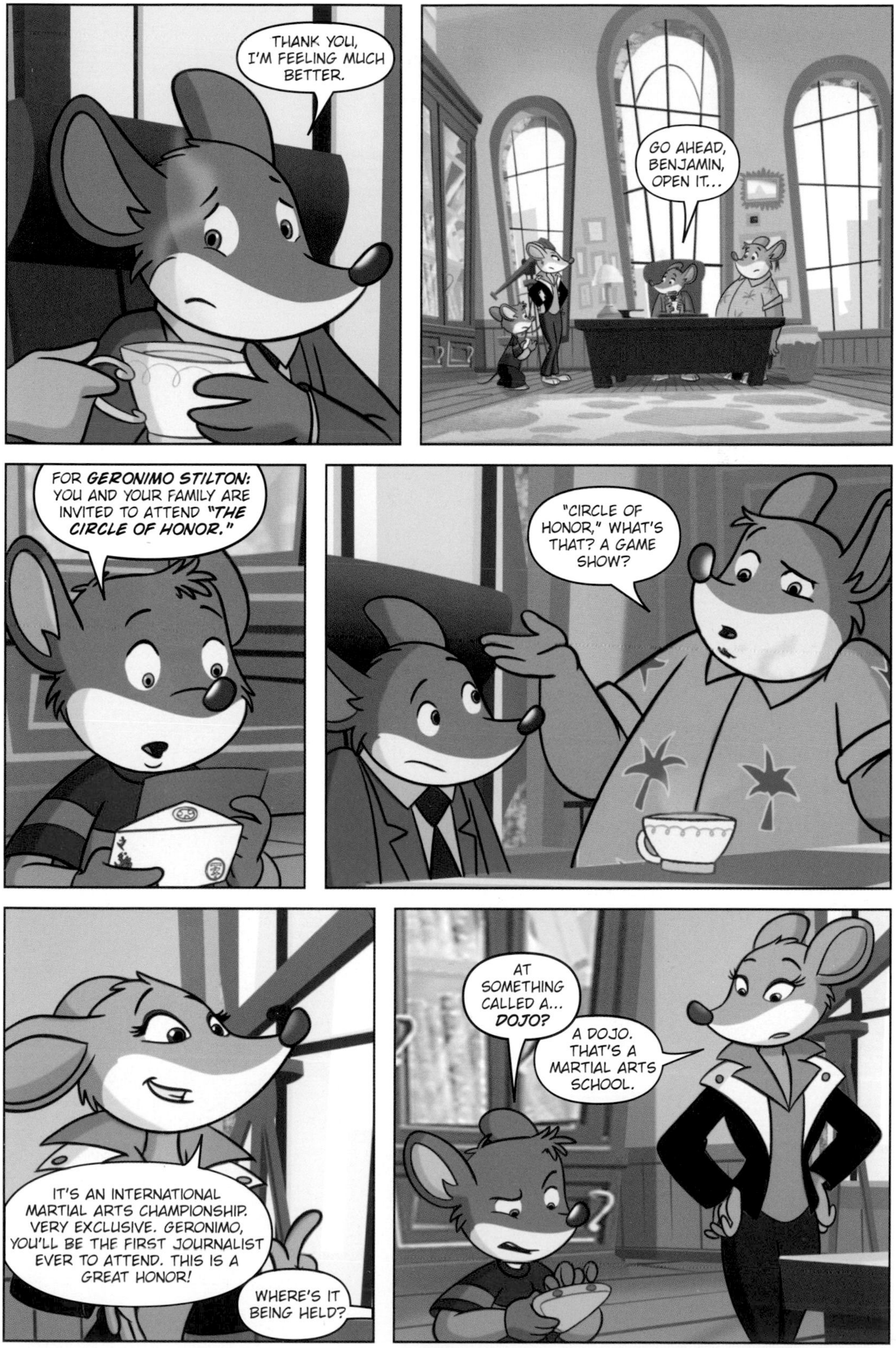
THANK YOU, I'M FEELING MUCH BETTER.
GO AHEAD, BENJAMIN, OPEN IT...
FOR GERONIMO STILTON: YOU AND YOUR FAMILY ARE INVITED TO ATTEND "THE CIRCLE OF HONOR."
"CIRCLE OF HONOR," WHAT'S THAT? A GAME SHOW?
IT'S AN INTERNATIONAL MARTIAL ARTS CHAMPIONSHIP. VERY EXCLUSIVE. GERONIMO, YOU'LL BE THE FIRST JOURNALIST EVER TO ATTEND. THIS IS A GREAT HONOR!
WHERE'S IT BEING HELD?
AT SOMETHING CALLED A... DOJO?
A DOJO. THAT'S A MARTIAL ARTS SCHOOL.

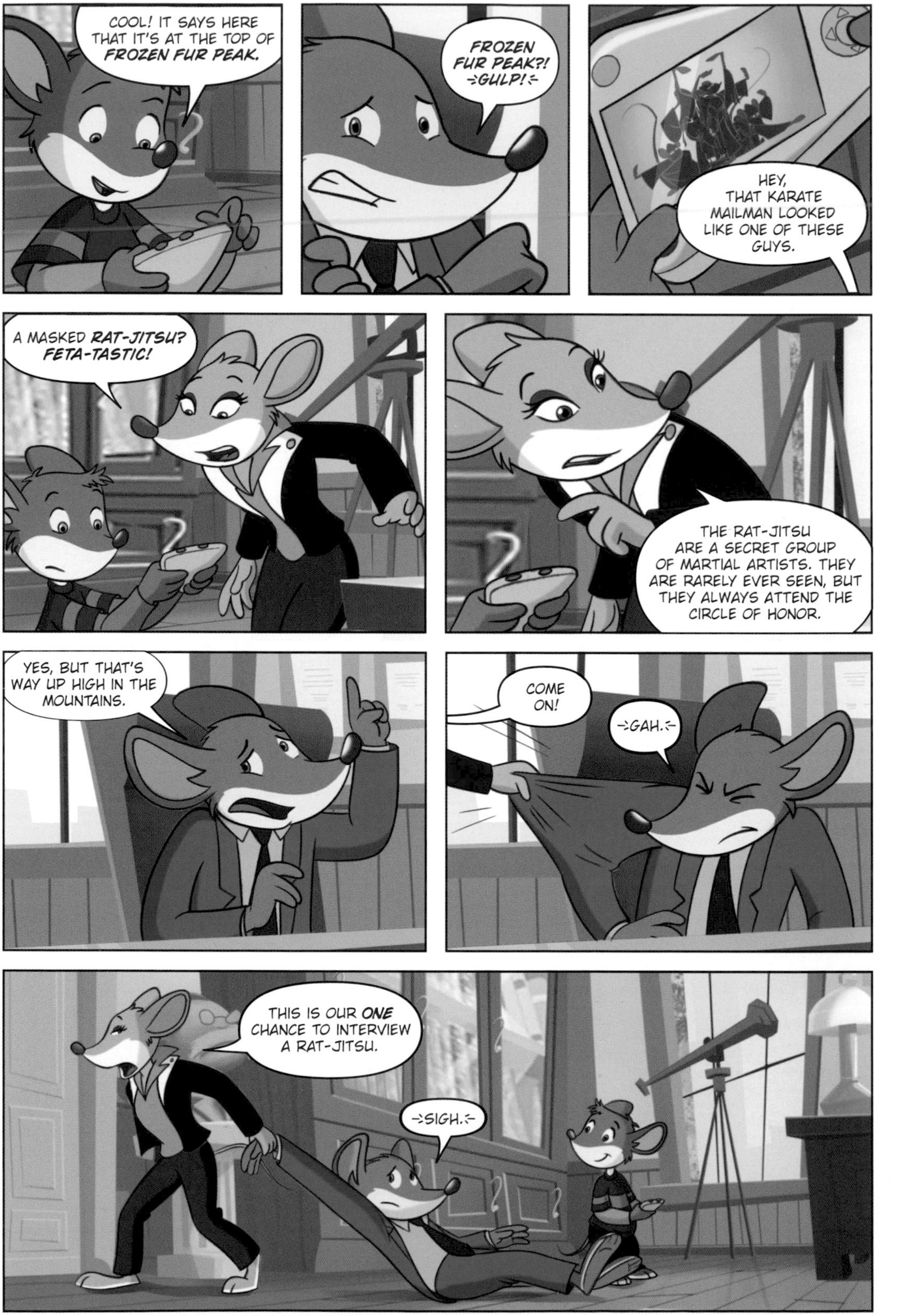
COOL! IT SAYS HERE THAT IT'S AT THE TOP OF FROZEN FUR PEAK.
FROZEN FUR PEAK?! -GULP!-
HEY, THAT KARATE MAILMAN LOOKED LIKE ONE OF THESE GUYS.
A MASKED RAT-JITSU? FETA-TASTIC!
THE RAT-JITSU ARE A SECRET GROUP OF MARTIAL ARTISTS. THEY ARE RARELY EVER SEEN, BUT THEY ALWAYS ATTEND THE CIRCLE OF HONOR.
YES, BUT THAT'S WAY UP HIGH IN THE MOUNTAINS.
COME ON!
-GAH.-
THIS IS OUR ONE CHANCE TO INTERVIEW A RAT-JITSU.
-SIGH.-

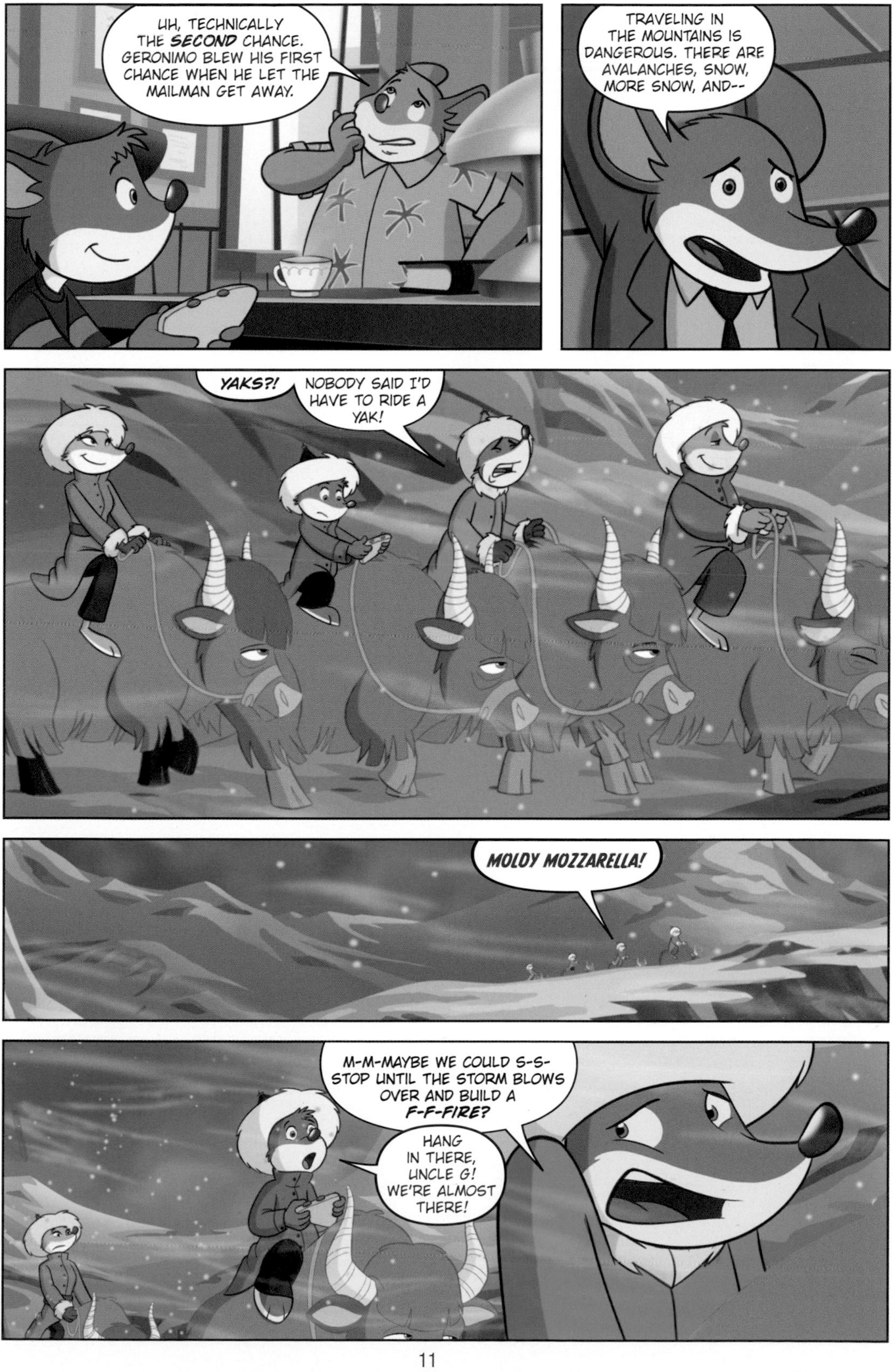
UH, TECHNICALLY THE **SECOND** CHANCE. GERONIMO BLEW HIS FIRST CHANCE WHEN HE LET THE MAILMAN GET AWAY.
TRAVELING IN THE MOUNTAINS IS DANGEROUS. THERE ARE AVALANCHES, SNOW, MORE SNOW, AND--
YAKS?!
NOBODY SAID I'D HAVE TO RIDE A YAK!
MOLDY MOZZARELLA!
M-M-MAYBE WE COULD S-S-STOP UNTIL THE STORM BLOWS OVER AND BUILD A **F-F-FIRE?**
HANG IN THERE, UNCLE G! WE'RE ALMOST THERE!

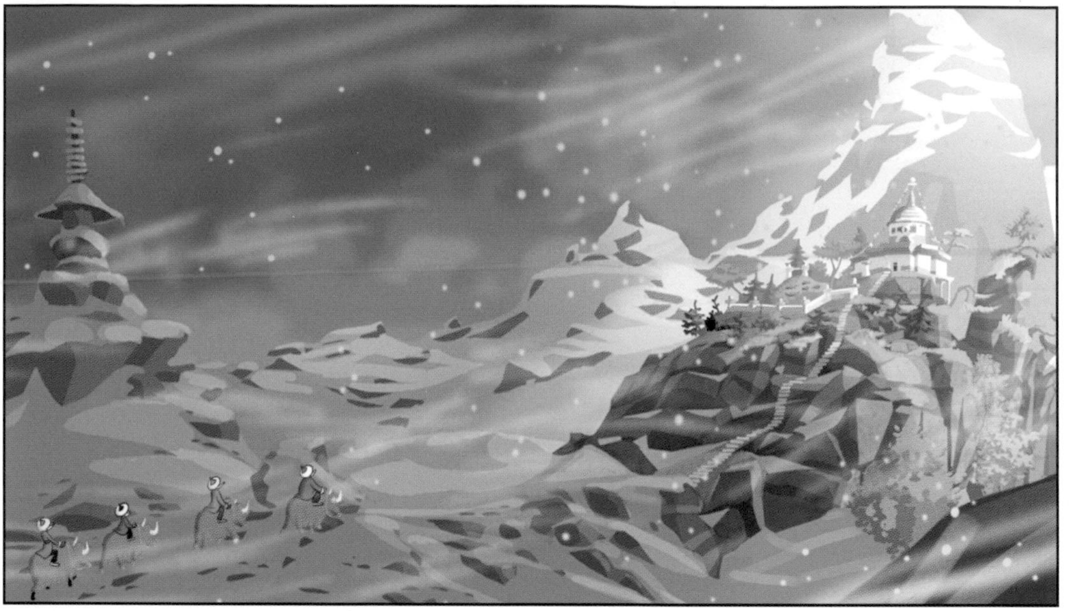

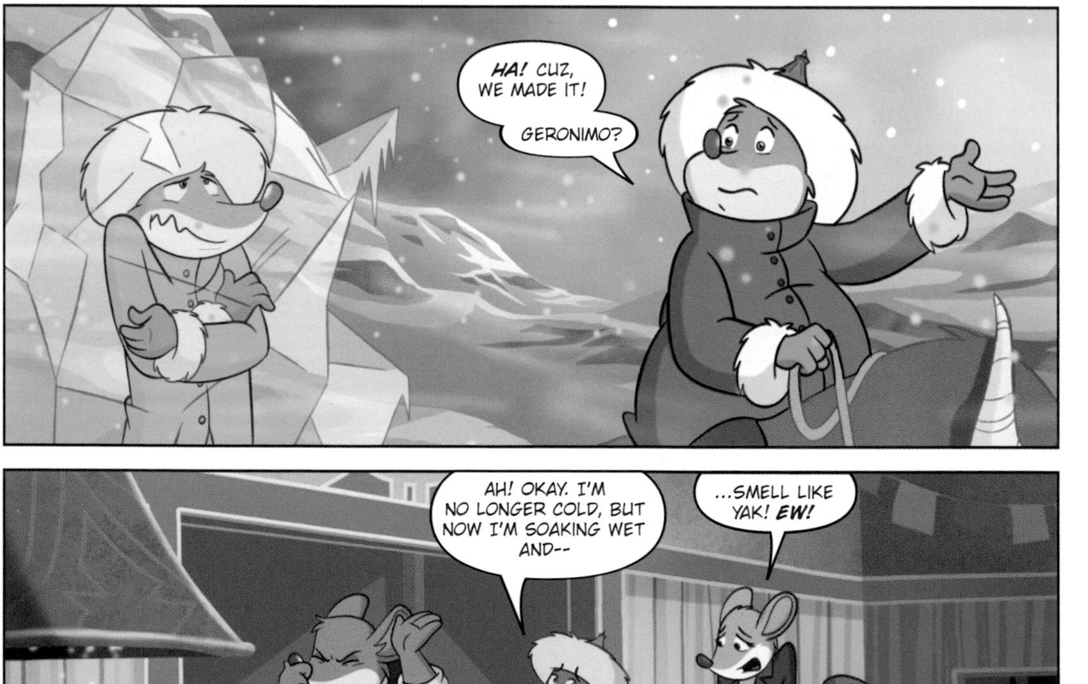
HA! CUZ, WE MADE IT!
GERONIMO?

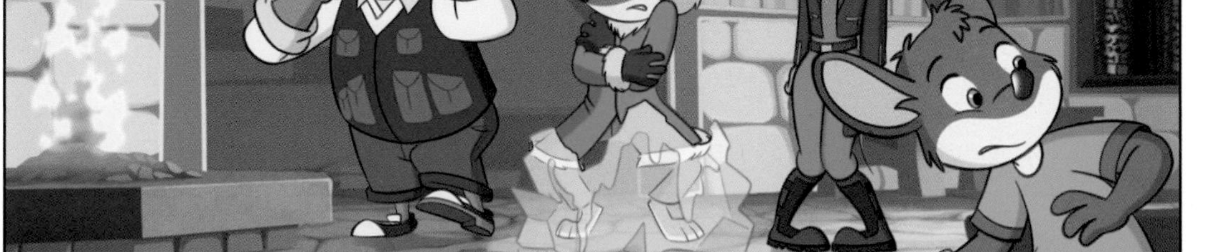
AH! OKAY. I'M NO LONGER COLD, BUT NOW I'M SOAKING WET AND--
...SMELL LIKE YAK! EW!

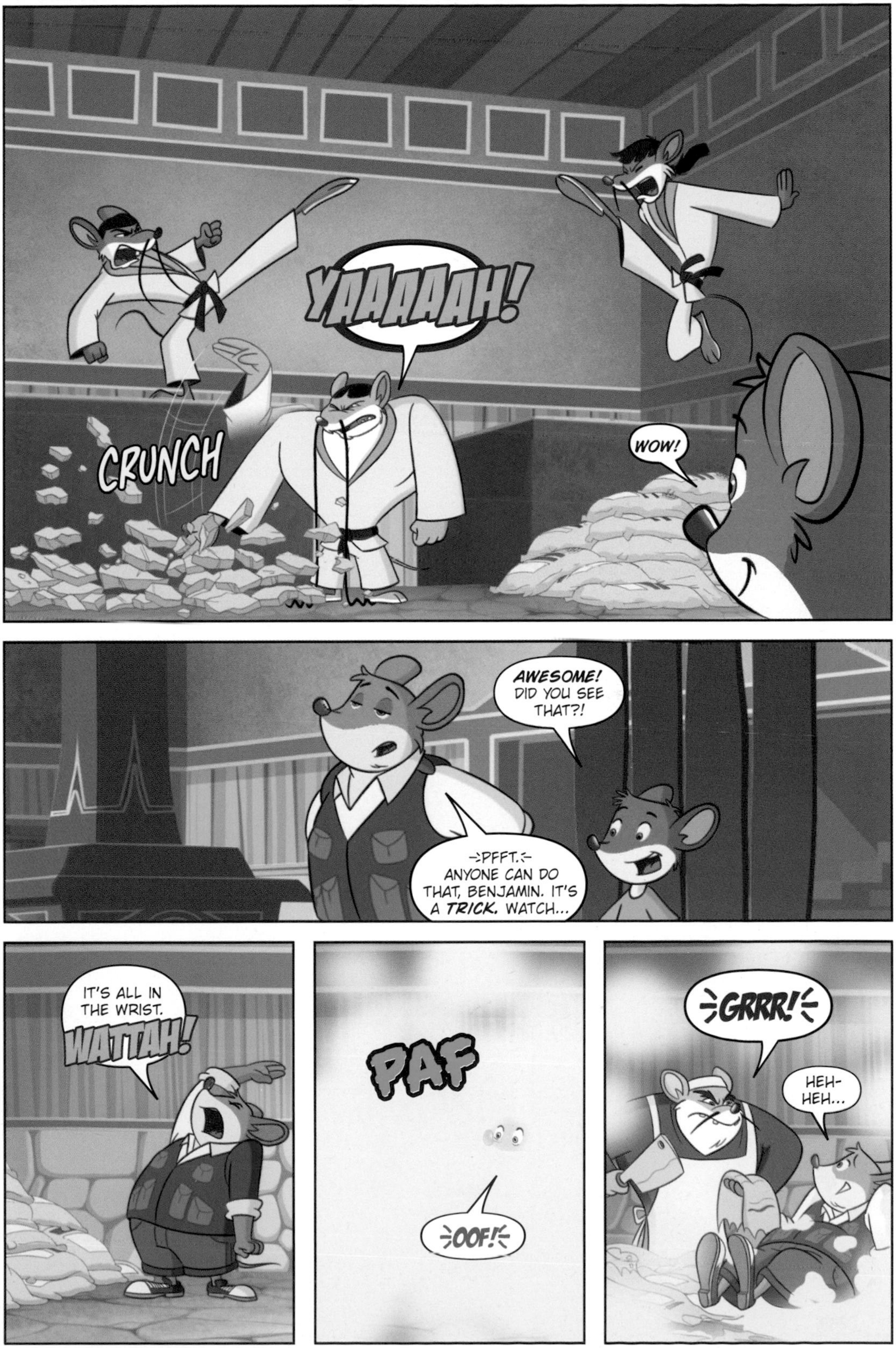
YAAAAAH!
CRUNCH
WOW!
AWESOME! DID YOU SEE THAT?!
PFFT. ANYONE CAN DO THAT, BENJAMIN. IT'S A TRICK. WATCH...
IT'S ALL IN THE WRIST.
WATTAH!
PAF
OOF!
GRRR!
HEH-HEH...

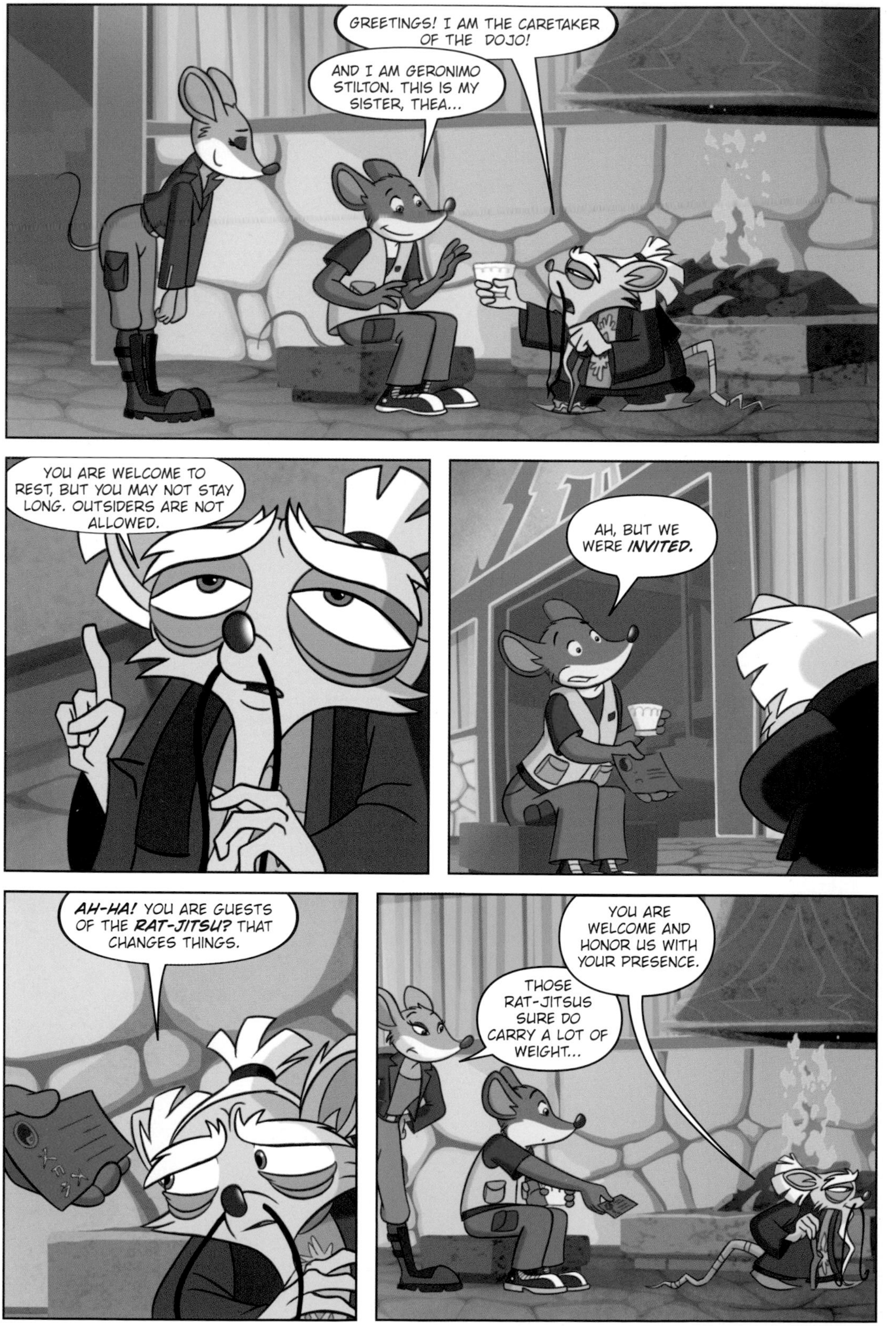
GREETINGS! I AM THE CARETAKER OF THE DOJO!
AND I AM GERONIMO STILTON. THIS IS MY SISTER, THEA...
YOU ARE WELCOME TO REST, BUT YOU MAY NOT STAY LONG. OUTSIDERS ARE NOT ALLOWED.
AH, BUT WE WERE INVITED.
AH-HA! YOU ARE GUESTS OF THE RAT-JITSU? THAT CHANGES THINGS.
YOU ARE WELCOME AND HONOR US WITH YOUR PRESENCE.
THOSE RAT-JITSUS SURE DO CARRY A LOT OF WEIGHT...

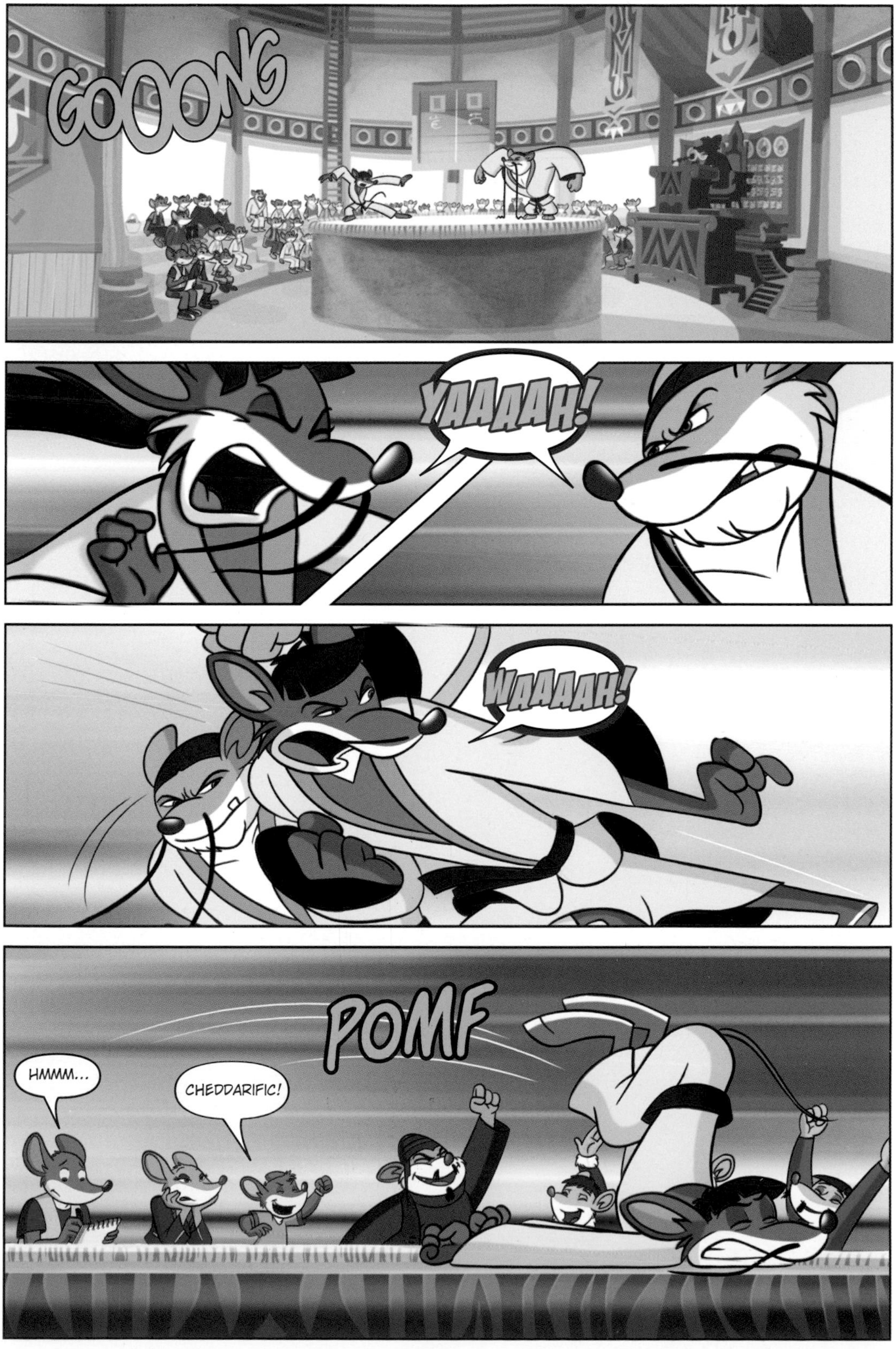
GOOONG
YAAAAH!
WAAAAH!
POMF
HMMM...
CHEDDARIFIC!

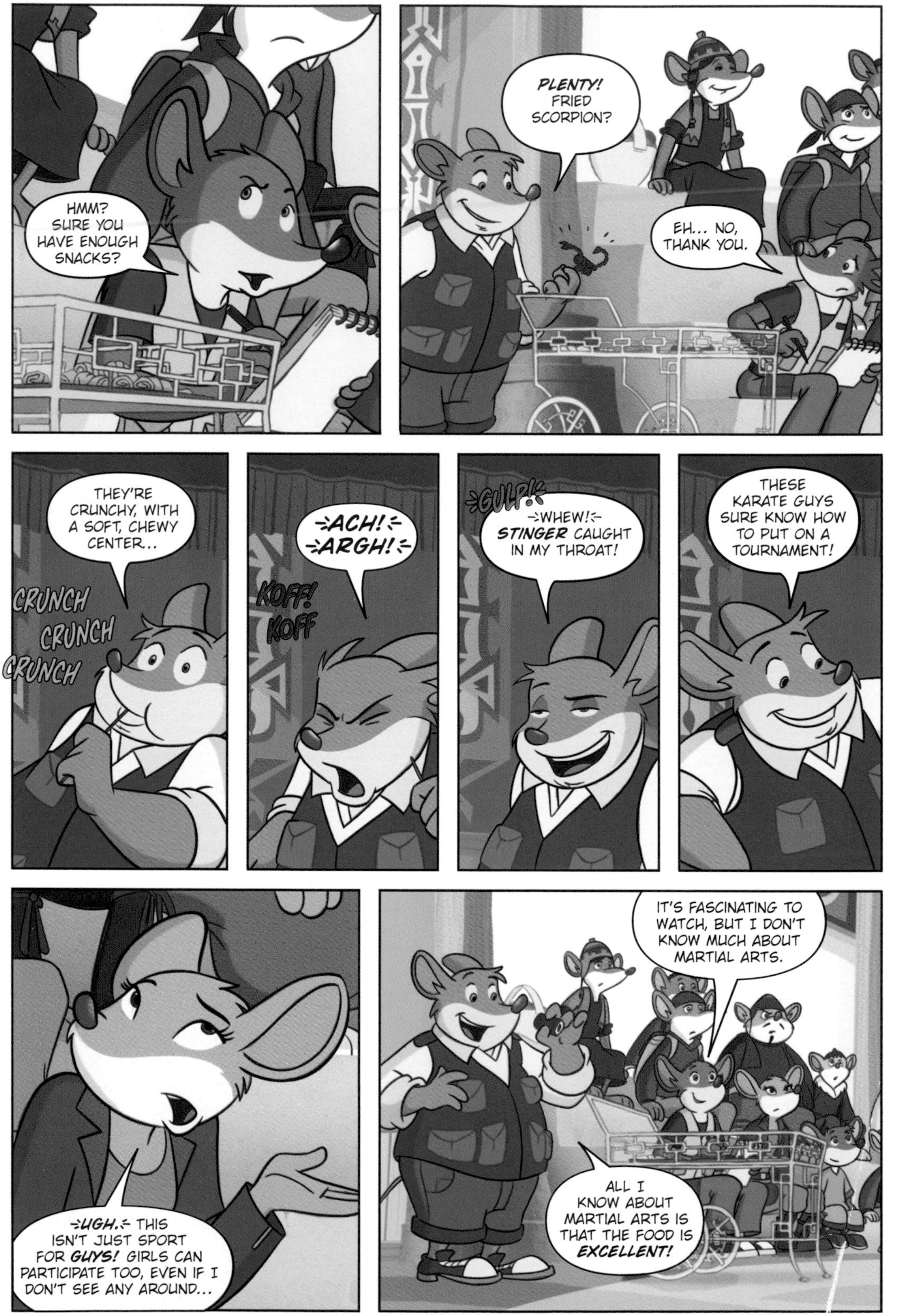
HMM? SURE YOU HAVE ENOUGH SNACKS?
PLENTY! FRIED SCORPION?
EH... NO, THANK YOU.
THEY'RE CRUNCHY, WITH A SOFT, CHEWY CENTER...
CRUNCH CRUNCH CRUNCH
ACH! ARGH!
KOFF! KOFF
GULP!
WHEW! STINGER CAUGHT IN MY THROAT!
THESE KARATE GUYS SURE KNOW HOW TO PUT ON A TOURNAMENT!
UGH. THIS ISN'T JUST SPORT FOR GUYS! GIRLS CAN PARTICIPATE TOO, EVEN IF I DON'T SEE ANY AROUND...
IT'S FASCINATING TO WATCH, BUT I DON'T KNOW MUCH ABOUT MARTIAL ARTS.
ALL I KNOW ABOUT MARTIAL ARTS IS THAT THE FOOD IS EXCELLENT!

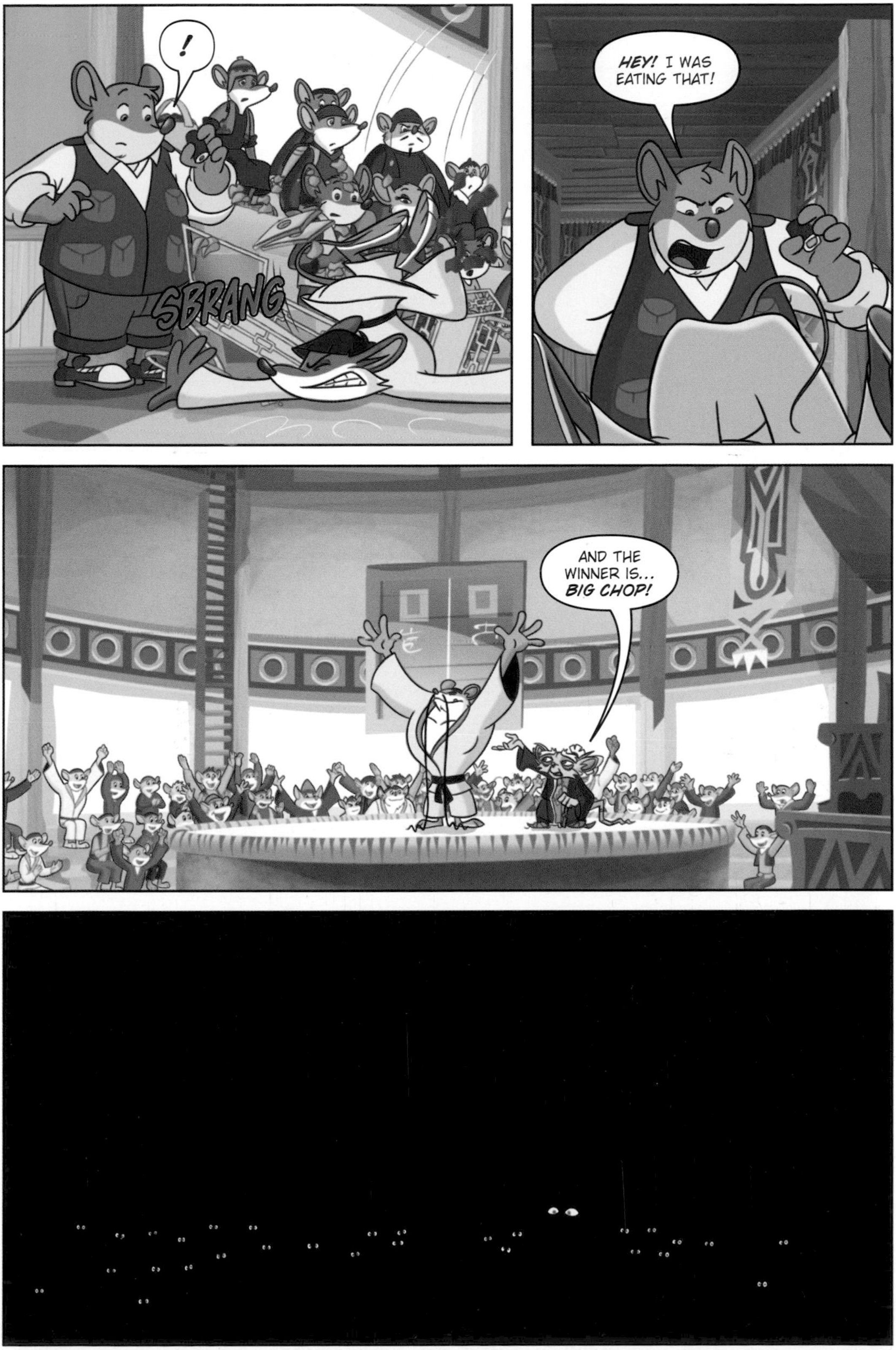
!
SBRANG
HEY! I WAS EATING THAT!
AND THE WINNER IS... BIG CHOP!

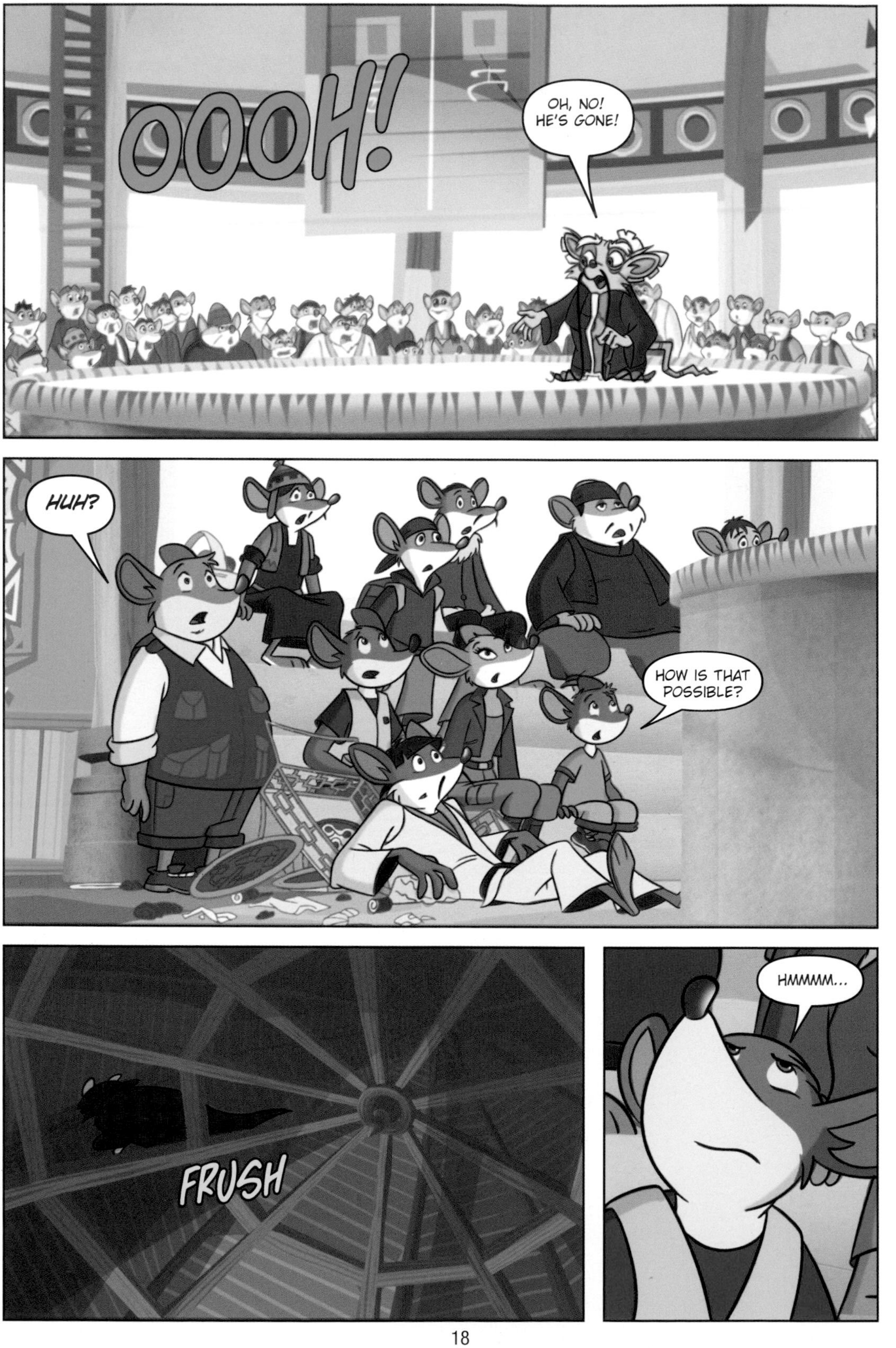
OOOH!
OH, NO! HE'S GONE!
HUH?
HOW IS THAT POSSIBLE?
FRUSH
HMMMM...

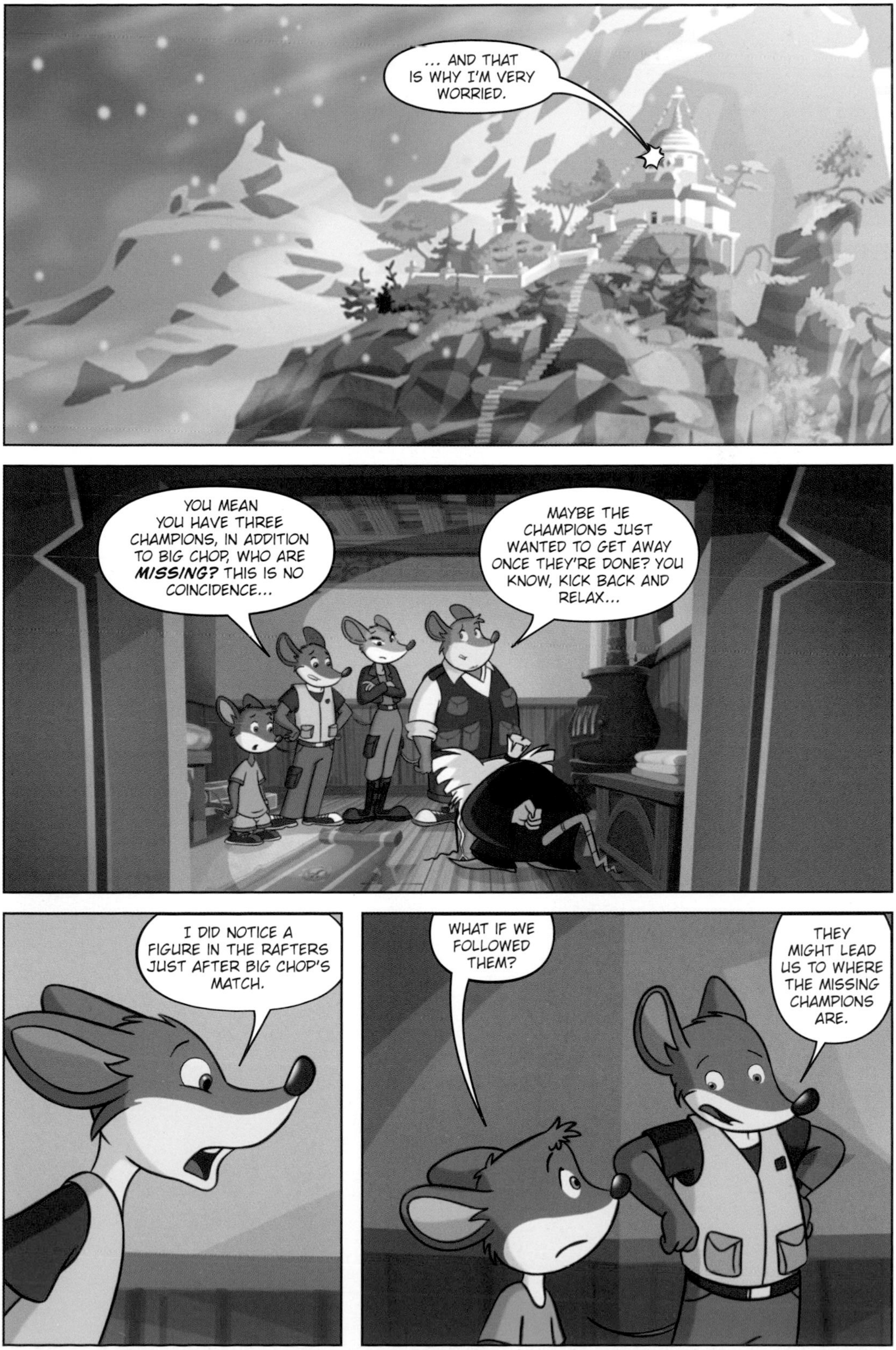
... AND THAT IS WHY I'M VERY WORRIED.
YOU MEAN YOU HAVE THREE CHAMPIONS, IN ADDITION TO BIG CHOP, WHO ARE ***MISSING?*** THIS IS NO COINCIDENCE...
MAYBE THE CHAMPIONS JUST WANTED TO GET AWAY ONCE THEY'RE DONE? YOU KNOW, KICK BACK AND RELAX...
I DID NOTICE A FIGURE IN THE RAFTERS JUST AFTER BIG CHOP'S MATCH.
WHAT IF WE FOLLOWED THEM?
THEY MIGHT LEAD US TO WHERE THE MISSING CHAMPIONS ARE.

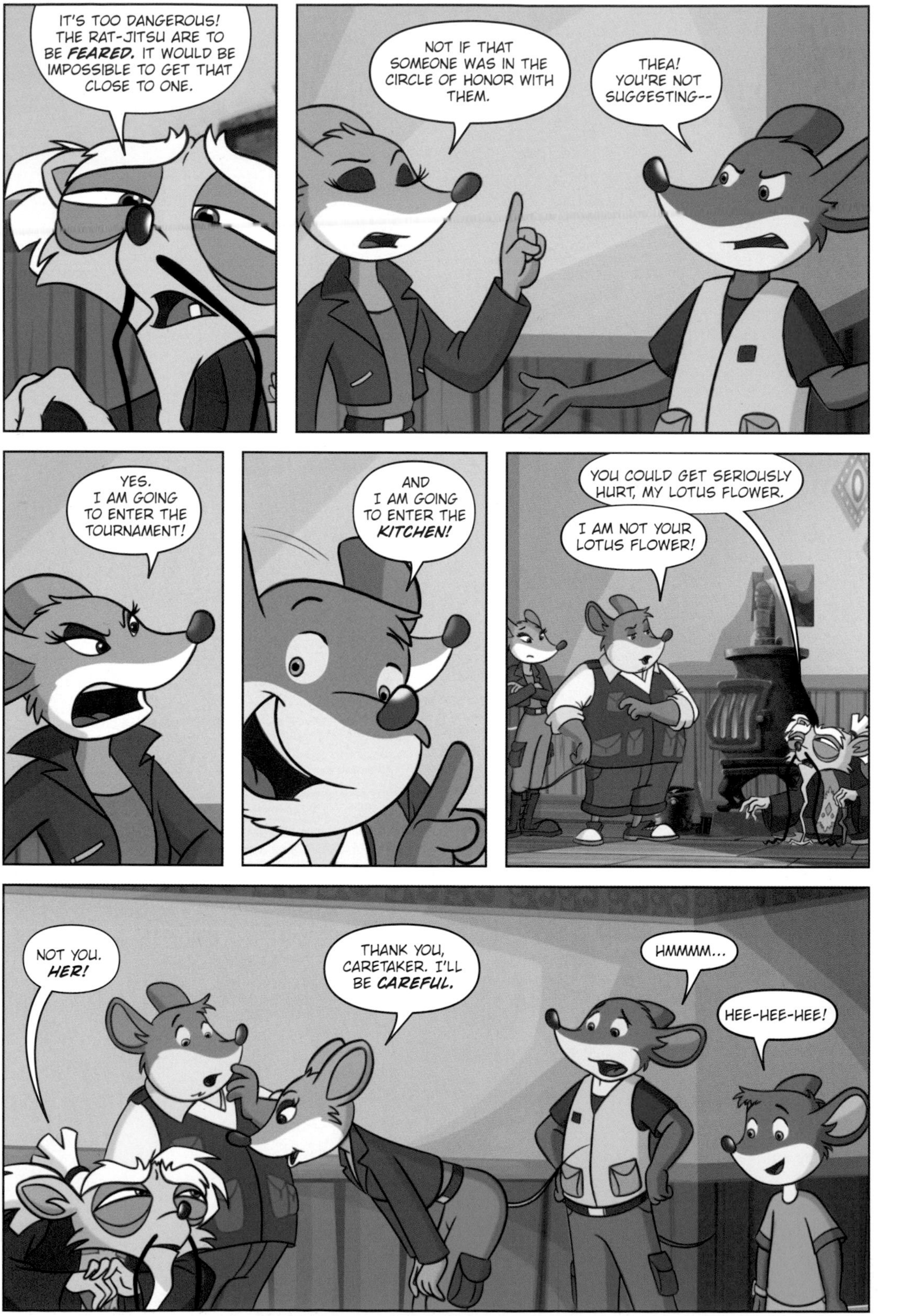
IT'S TOO DANGEROUS! THE RAT-JITSU ARE TO BE FEARED. IT WOULD BE IMPOSSIBLE TO GET THAT CLOSE TO ONE.
NOT IF THAT SOMEONE WAS IN THE CIRCLE OF HONOR WITH THEM.
THEA! YOU'RE NOT SUGGESTING--
YES. I AM GOING TO ENTER THE TOURNAMENT!
AND I AM GOING TO ENTER THE KITCHEN!
YOU COULD GET SERIOUSLY HURT, MY LOTUS FLOWER.
I AM NOT YOUR LOTUS FLOWER!
NOT YOU. HER!
THANK YOU, CARETAKER. I'LL BE CAREFUL.
HMMMM...
HEE-HEE-HEE!

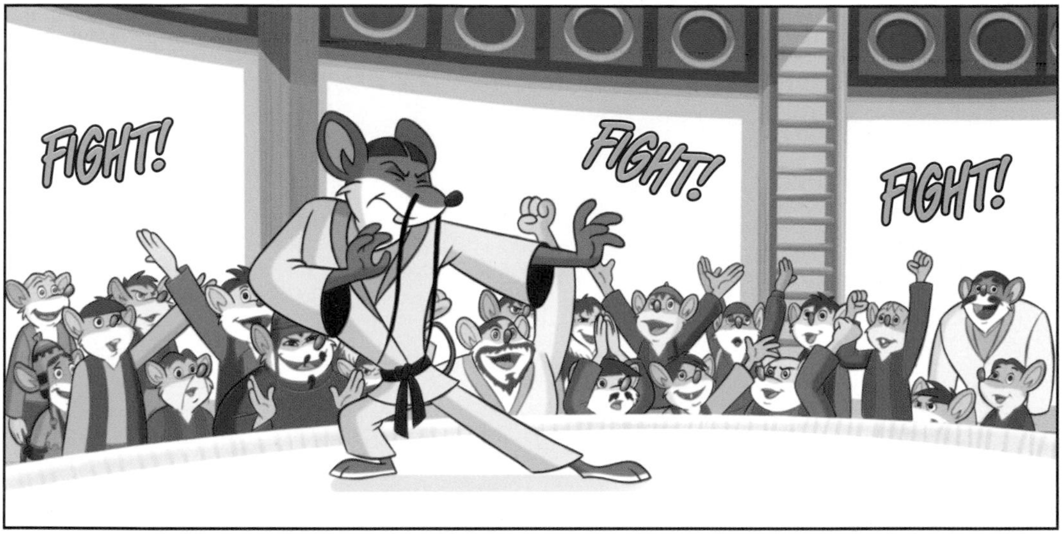
FIGHT!
FIGHT!
FIGHT!

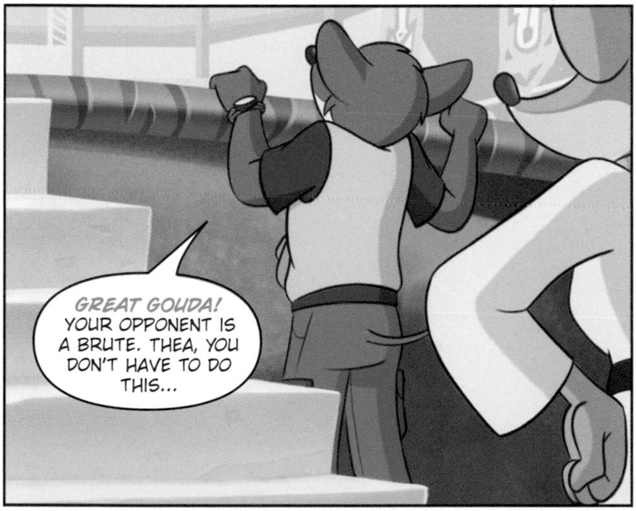
GREAT GOUDA! YOUR OPPONENT IS A BRUTE. THEA, YOU DON'T HAVE TO DO THIS...

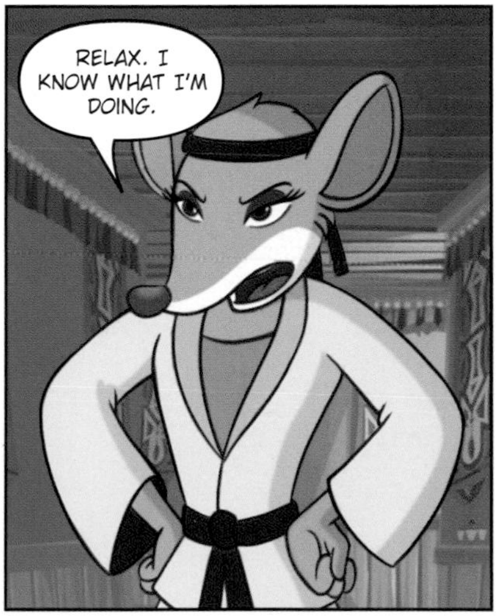
RELAX. I KNOW WHAT I'M DOING.

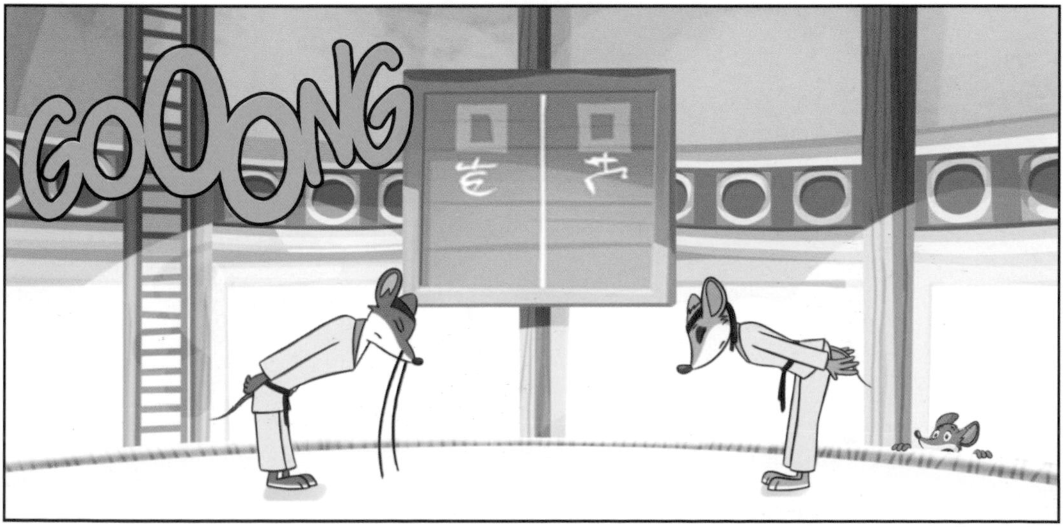
GOOONG

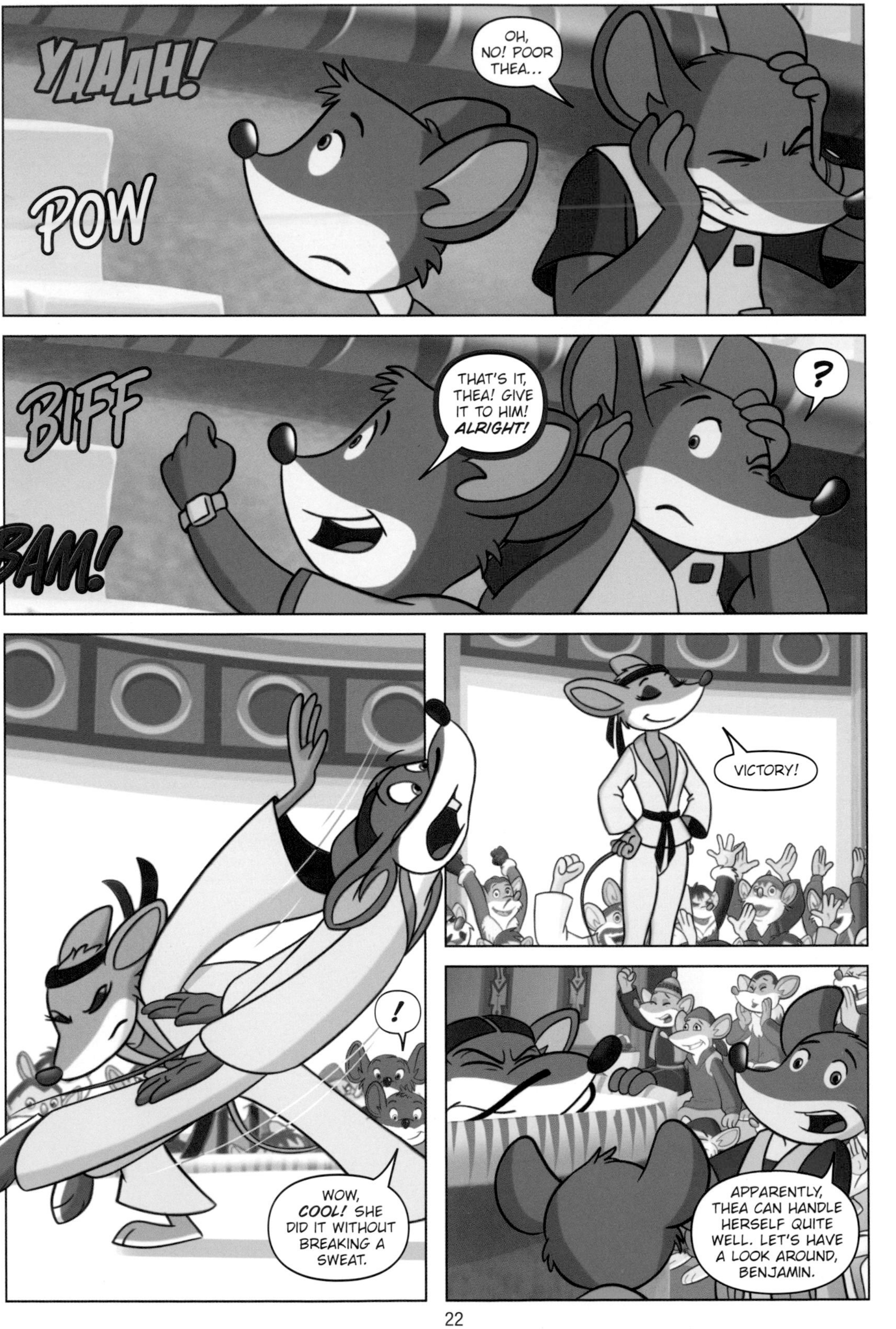
YAAAH!
POW
OH, NO! POOR THEA...
BIFF
BAM!
THAT'S IT, THEA! GIVE IT TO HIM! ALRIGHT!
?
!
WOW, COOL! SHE DID IT WITHOUT BREAKING A SWEAT.
VICTORY!
APPARENTLY, THEA CAN HANDLE HERSELF QUITE WELL. LET'S HAVE A LOOK AROUND, BENJAMIN.

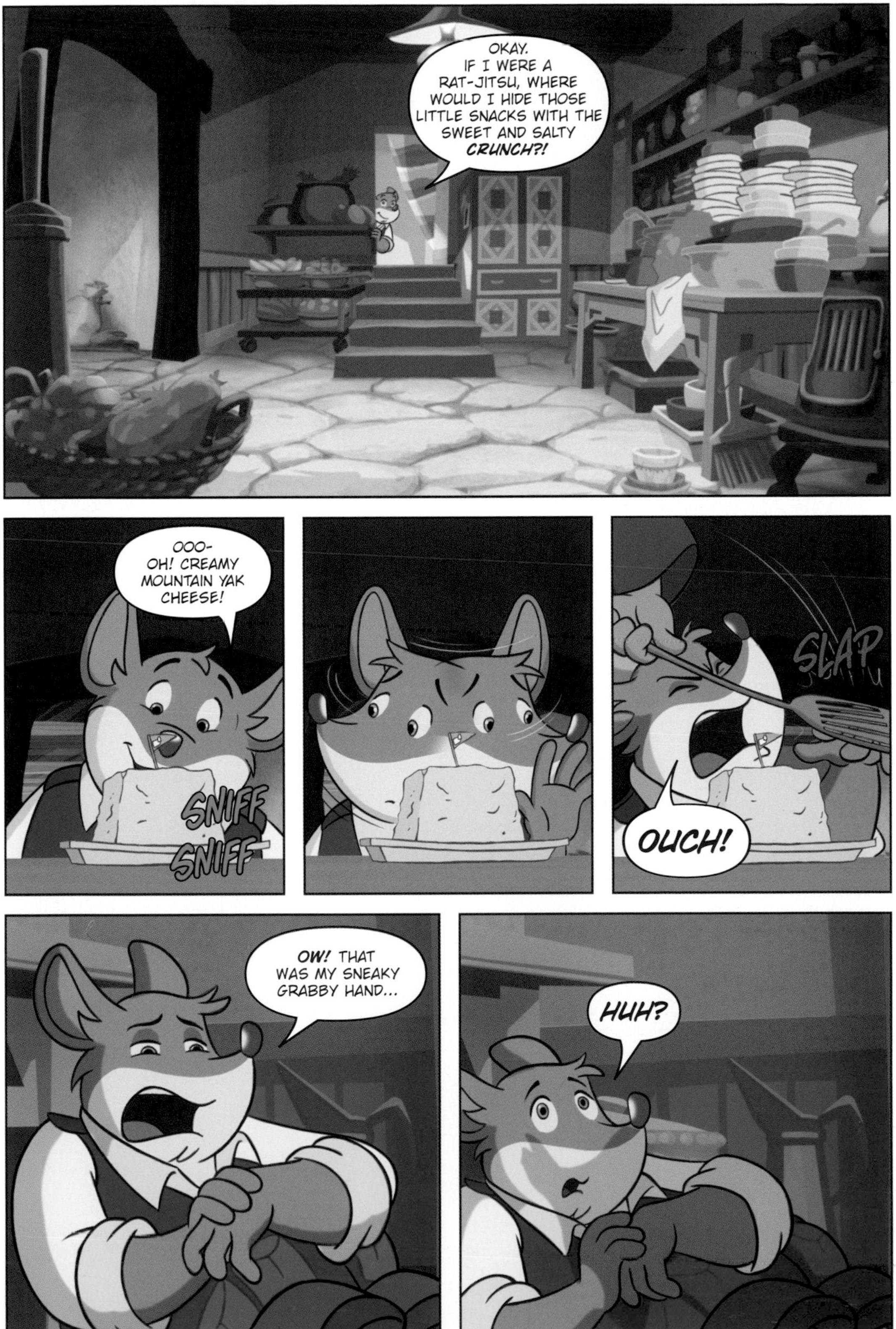

OKAY. IF I WERE A RAT-JITSU, WHERE WOULD I HIDE THOSE LITTLE SNACKS WITH THE SWEET AND SALTY **CRUNCH?!**
OOO- OH! CREAMY MOUNTAIN YAK CHEESE!
SNIFF SNIFF
SLAP
OUCH!
OW! THAT WAS MY SNEAKY GRABBY HAND...
HUH?

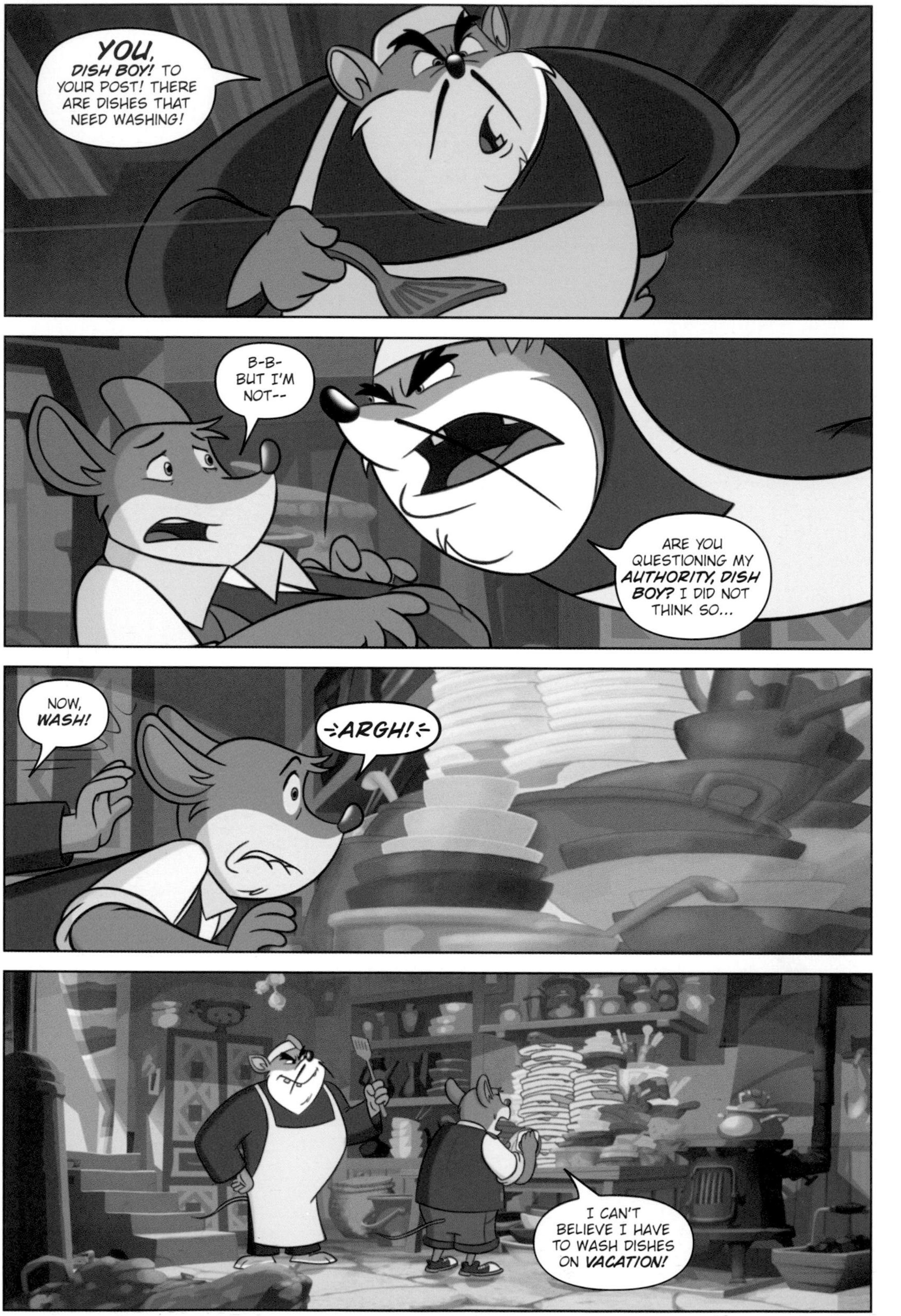
YOU, DISH BOY! TO YOUR POST! THERE ARE DISHES THAT NEED WASHING!
B-B- BUT I'M NOT--
ARE YOU QUESTIONING MY AUTHORITY, DISH BOY? I DID NOT THINK SO...
NOW, WASH!
ARGH!
I CAN'T BELIEVE I HAVE TO WASH DISHES ON VACATION!

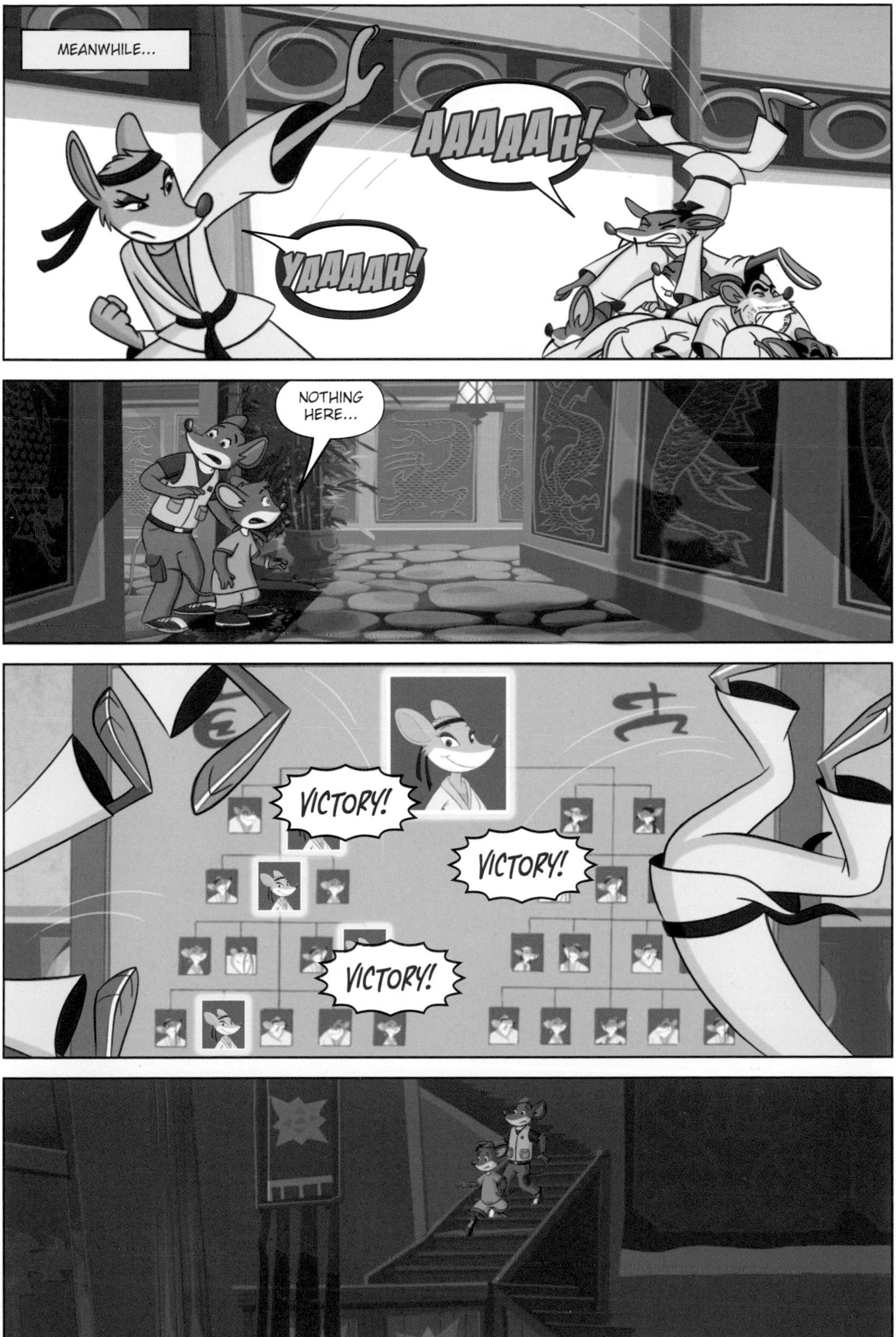
MEANWHILE...
YAAAAH!
AAAAAH!
NOTHING HERE...
VICTORY!
VICTORY!
VICTORY!

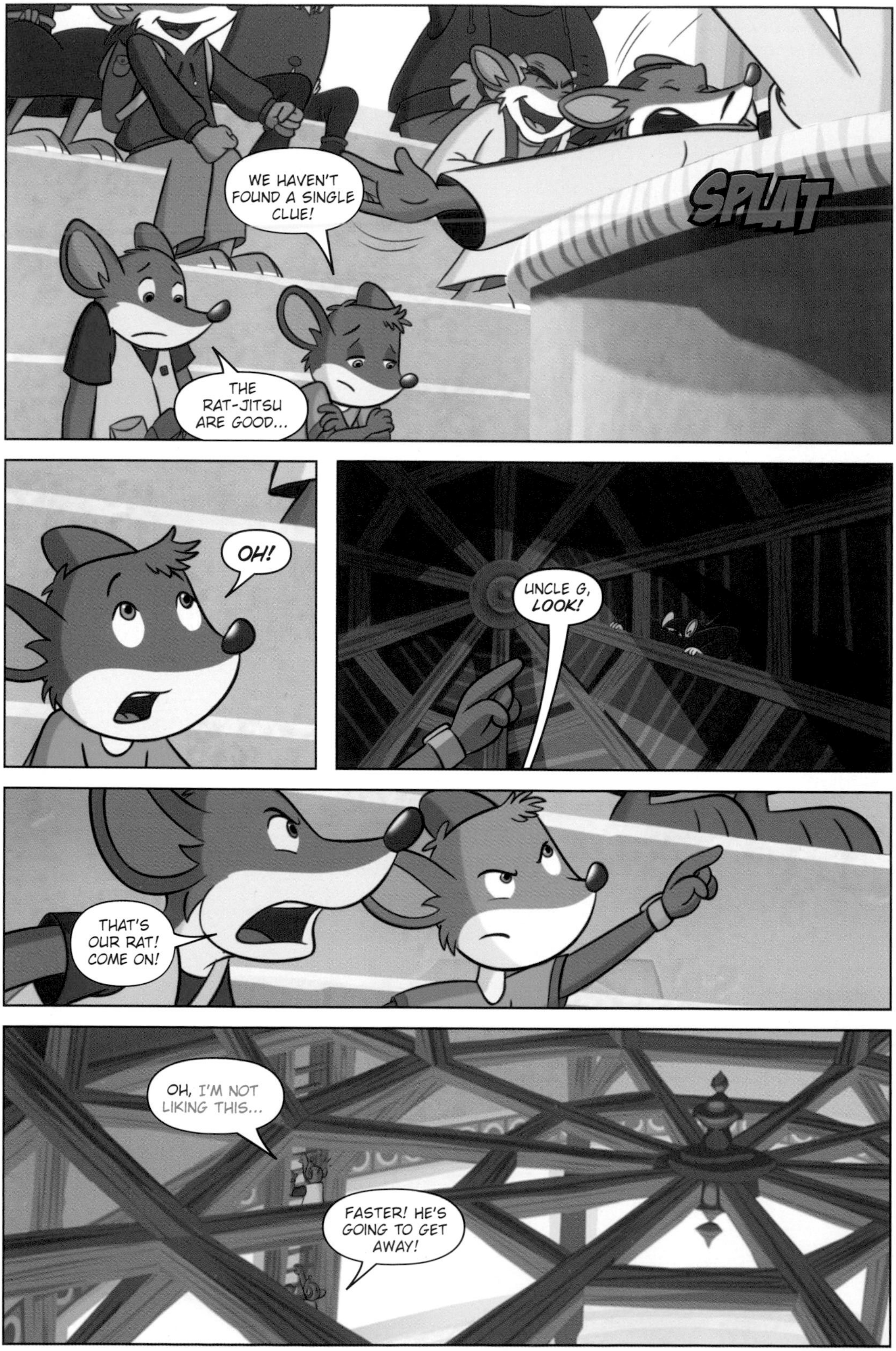
WE HAVEN'T FOUND A SINGLE CLUE!
SPLAT
THE RAT-JITSU ARE GOOD...
OH!
UNCLE G, LOOK!
THAT'S OUR RAT! COME ON!
OH, I'M NOT LIKING THIS...
FASTER! HE'S GOING TO GET AWAY!

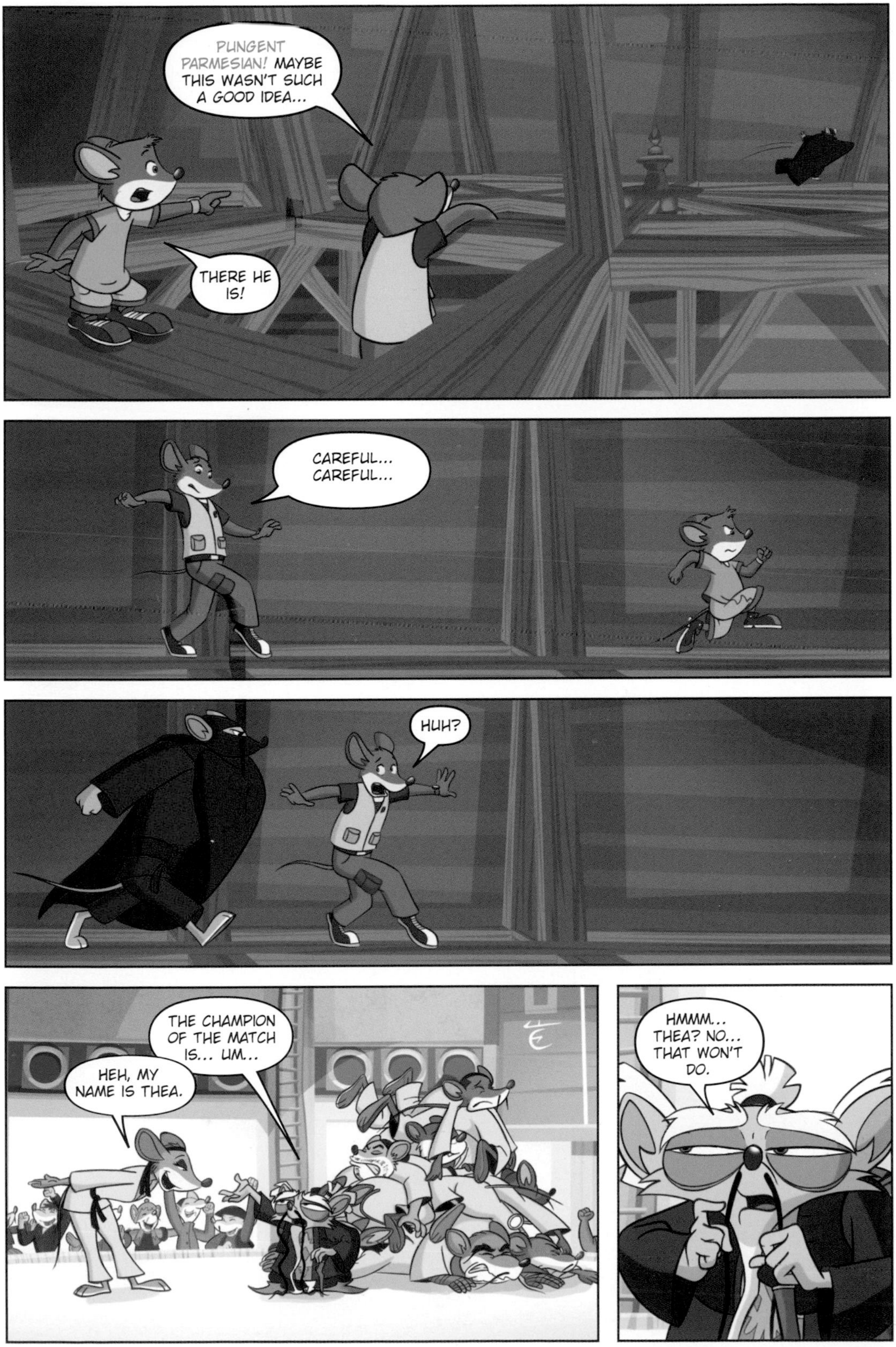
PUNGENT PARMESIAN! MAYBE THIS WASN'T SUCH A GOOD IDEA...
THERE HE IS!
CAREFUL... CAREFUL...
HUH?
THE CHAMPION OF THE MATCH IS... UM...
HEH, MY NAME IS THEA.
HMMM... THEA? NO... THAT WON'T DO.

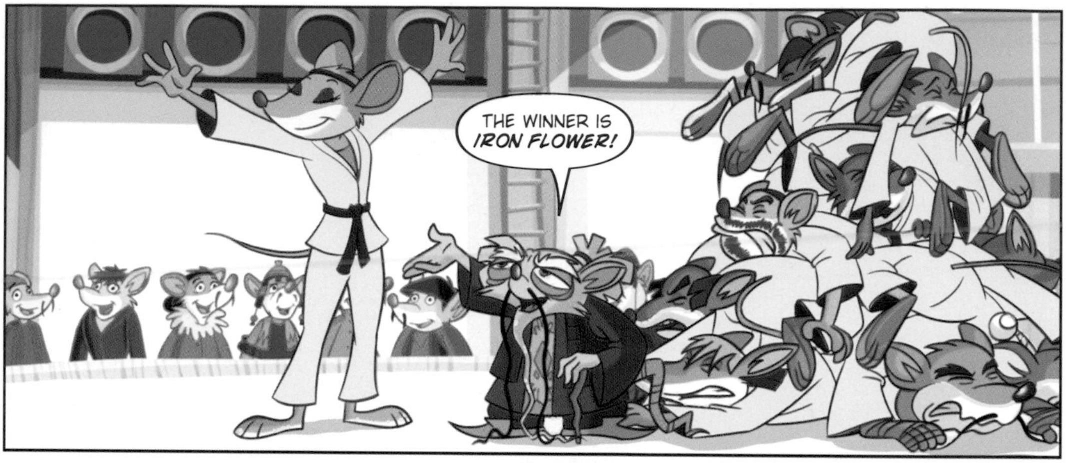
THE WINNER IS *IRON FLOWER!*

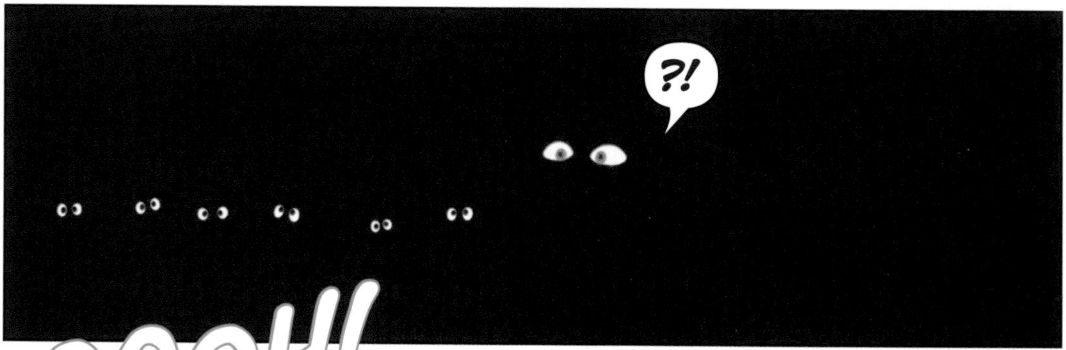
?!

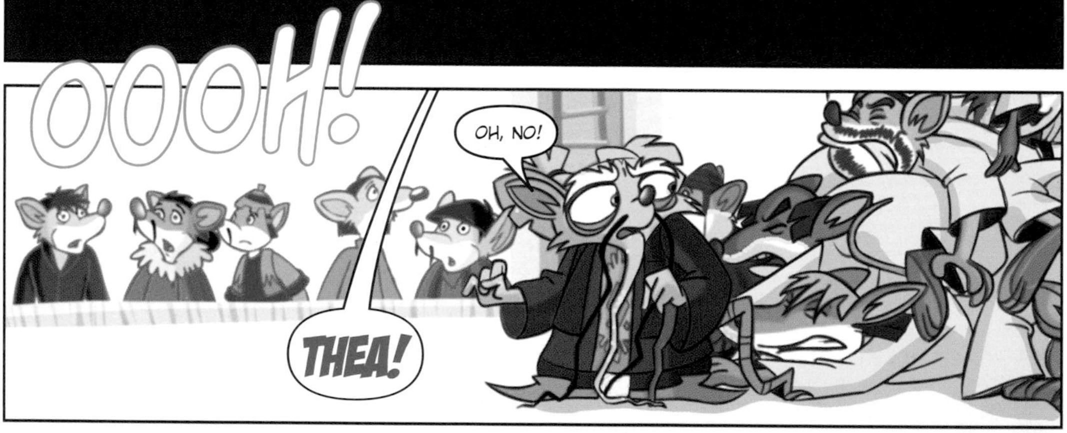
OOOH!
OH, NO!
THEA!

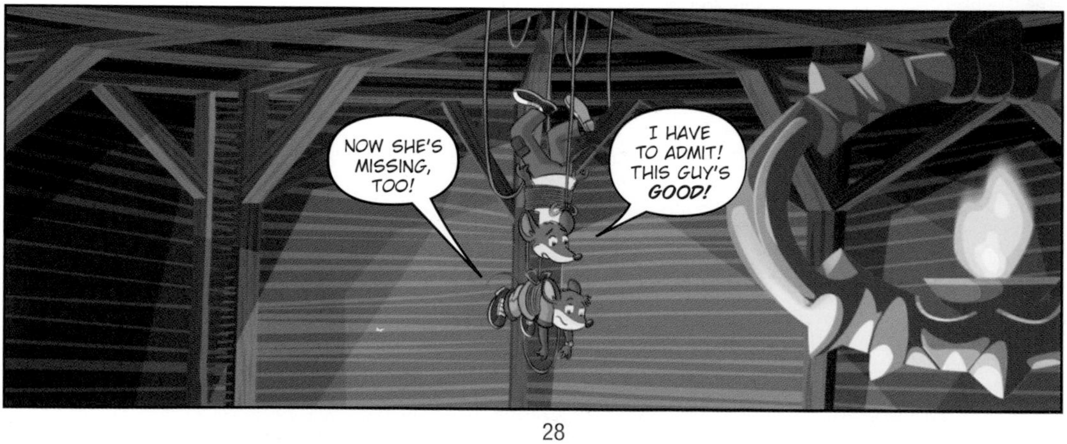
NOW SHE'S MISSING, TOO!
I HAVE TO ADMIT! THIS GUY'S *GOOD!*

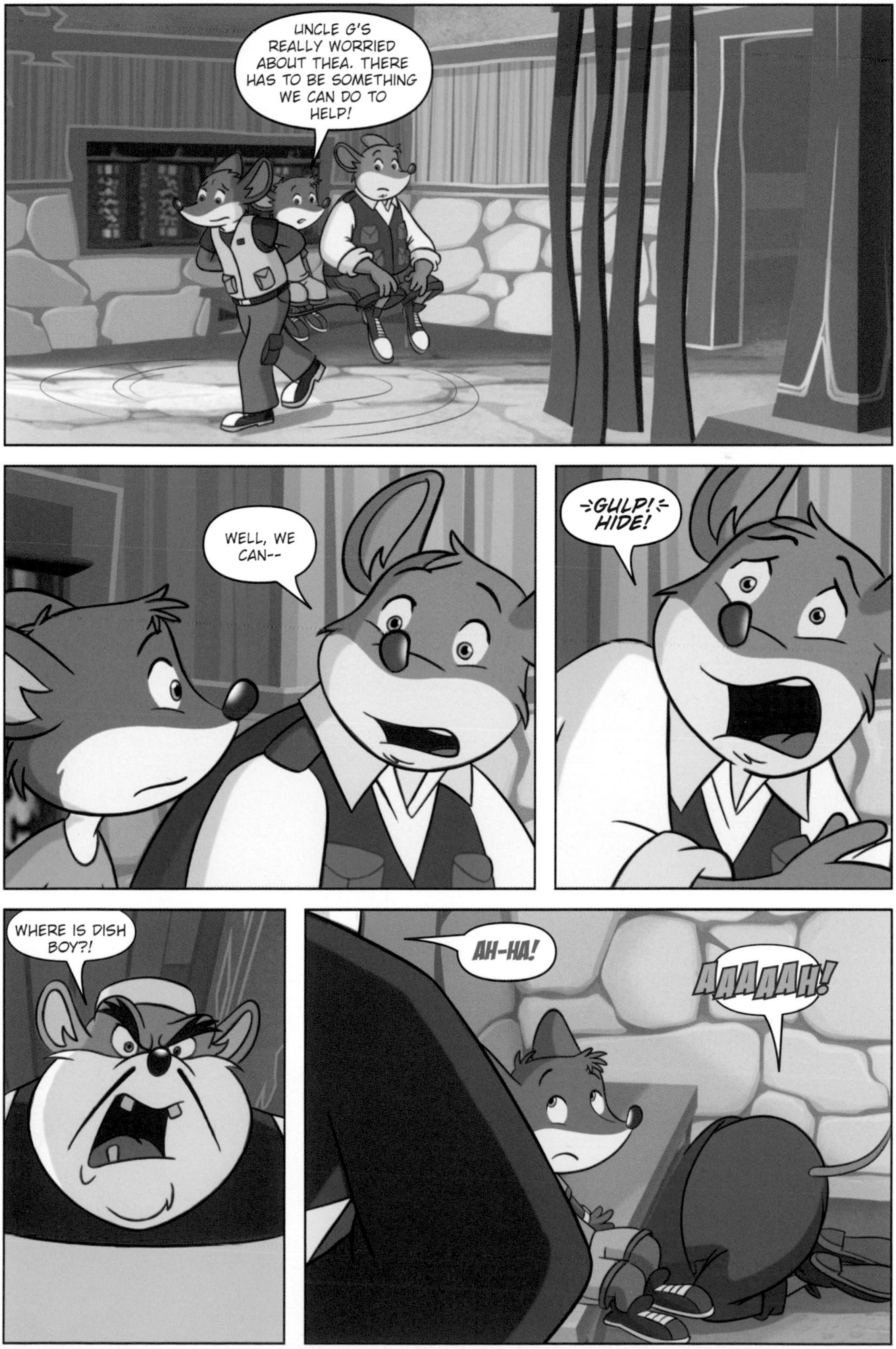
UNCLE G'S REALLY WORRIED ABOUT THEA. THERE HAS TO BE SOMETHING WE CAN DO TO HELP!
WELL, WE CAN--
GULP! HIDE!
WHERE IS DISH BOY?!
AH-HA!
AAAAAH!

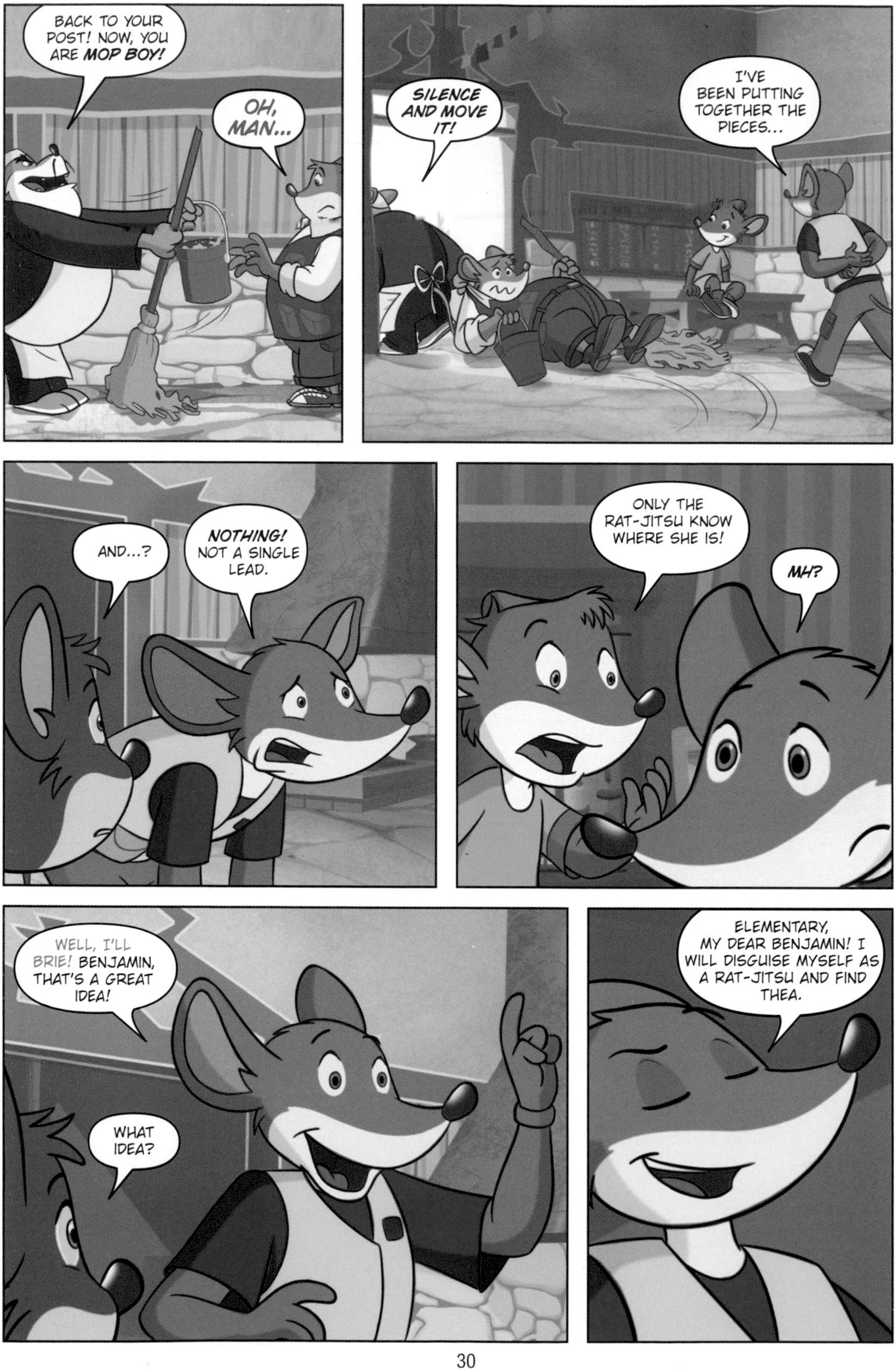
BACK TO YOUR POST! NOW, YOU ARE MOP BOY!
OH, MAN...
SILENCE AND MOVE IT!
I'VE BEEN PUTTING TOGETHER THE PIECES...
AND...?
NOTHING! NOT A SINGLE LEAD.
ONLY THE RAT-JITSU KNOW WHERE SHE IS!
MH?
WELL, I'LL BRIE! BENJAMIN, THAT'S A GREAT IDEA!
WHAT IDEA?
ELEMENTARY, MY DEAR BENJAMIN! I WILL DISGUISE MYSELF AS A RAT-JITSU AND FIND THEA.

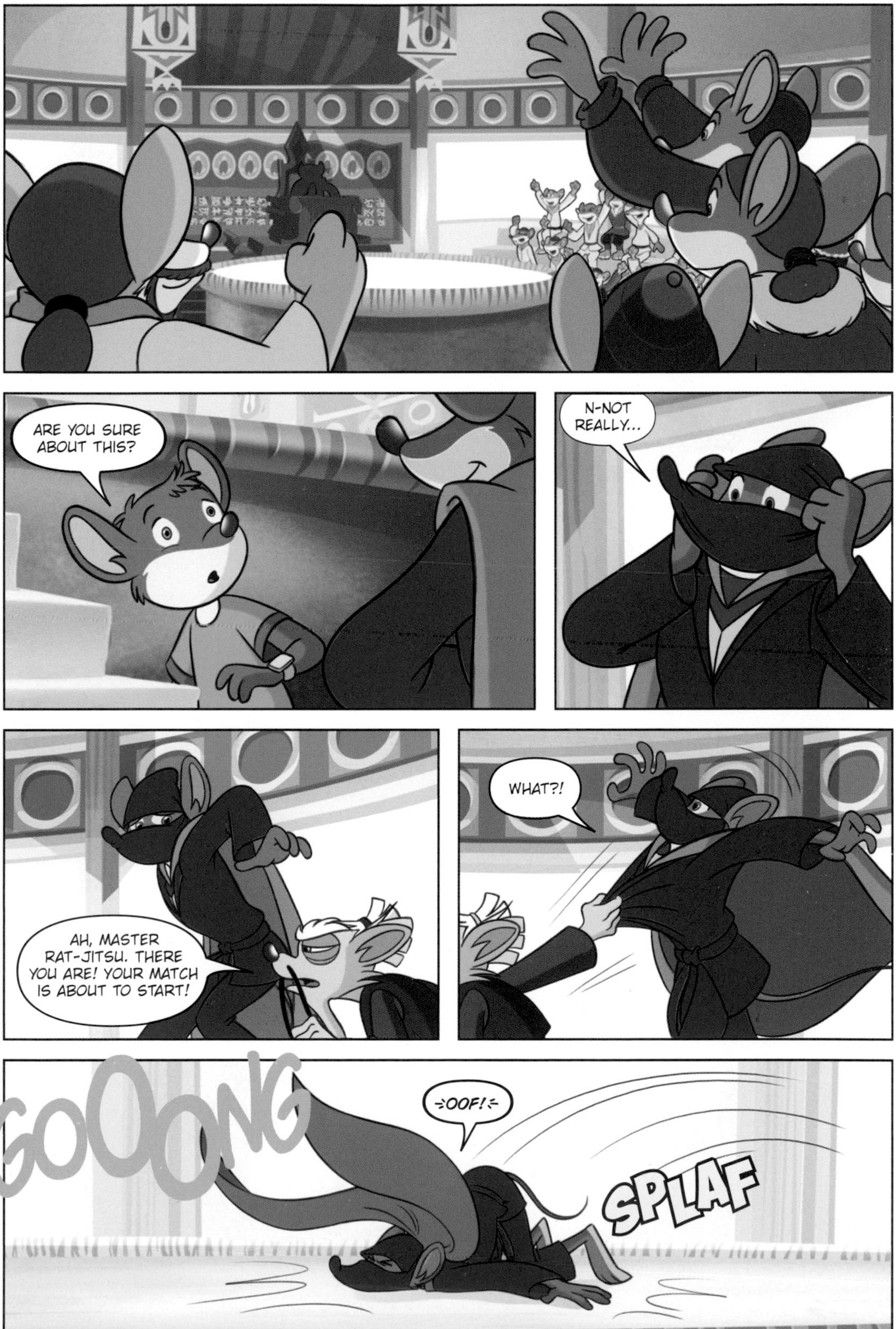
ARE YOU SURE ABOUT THIS?
N-NOT REALLY...
AH, MASTER RAT-JITSU. THERE YOU ARE! YOUR MATCH IS ABOUT TO START!
WHAT?!
GOOONG
OOF!
SPLAF

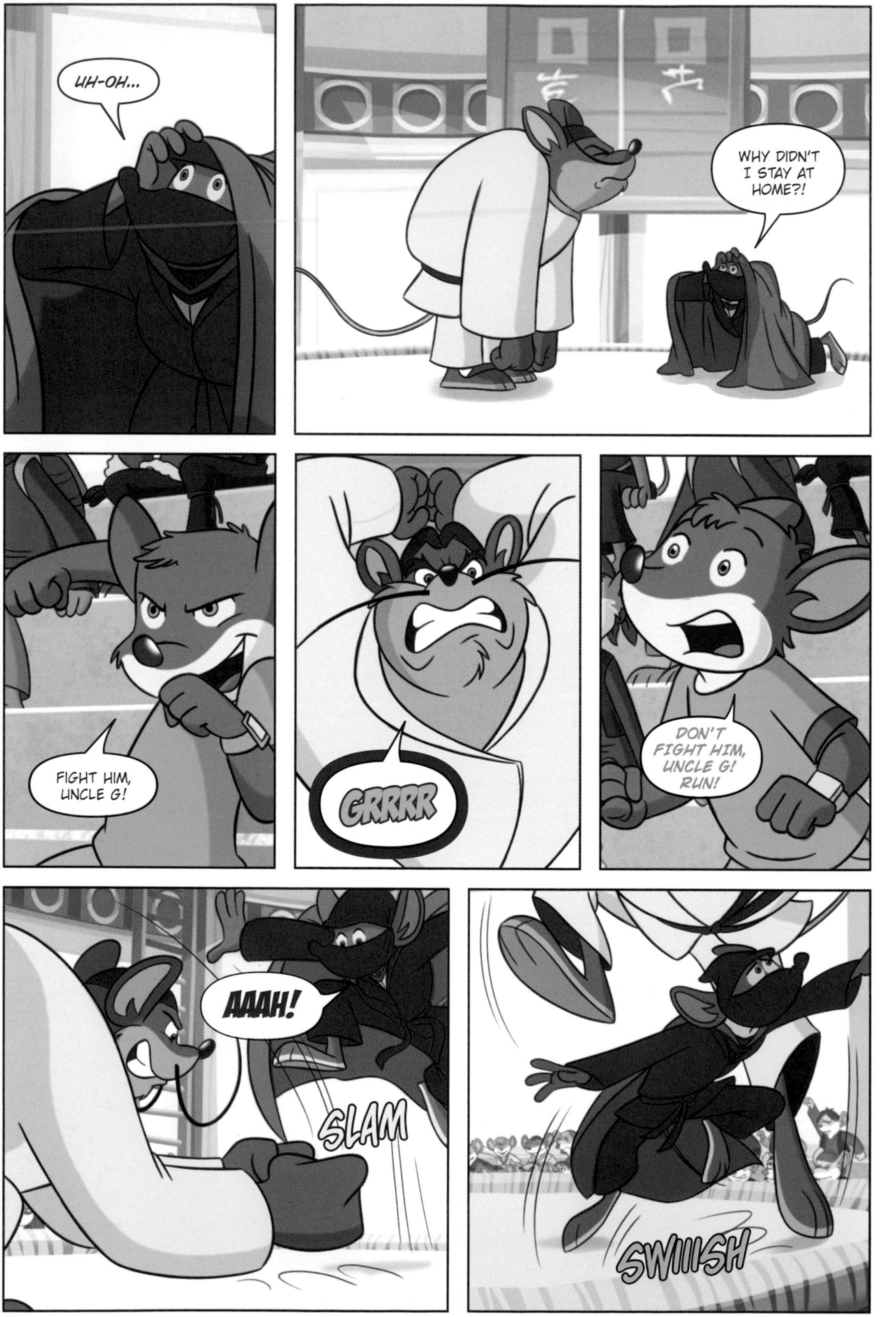
UH-OH...
WHY DIDN'T I STAY AT HOME?!
FIGHT HIM, UNCLE G!
GRRRR
DON'T FIGHT HIM, UNCLE G! RUN!
AAAH!
SLAM
SWIIISH

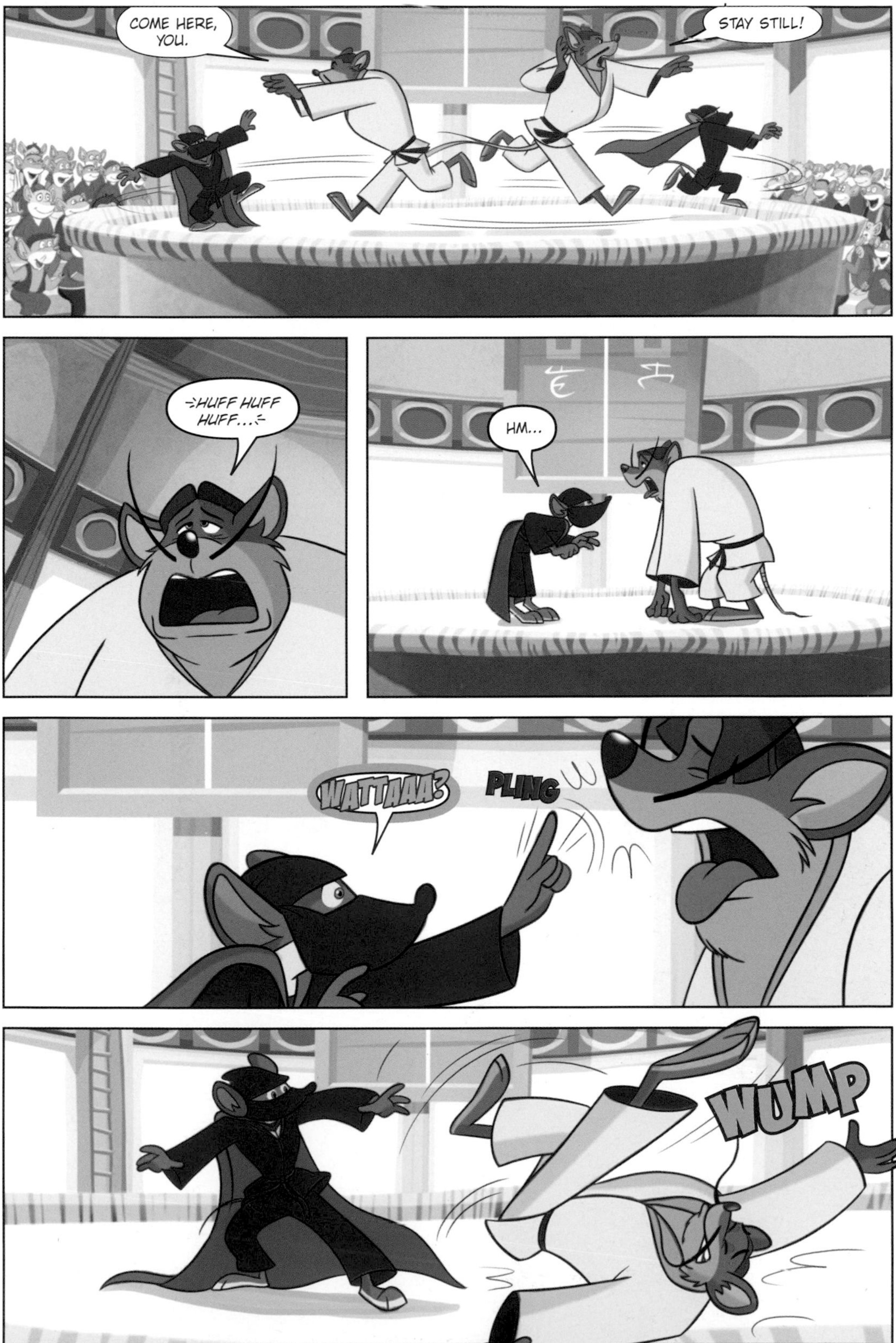
COME HERE, YOU.
STAY STILL!
HUFF HUFF HUFF...
HM...
WATTAAA?
PLING
WUMP

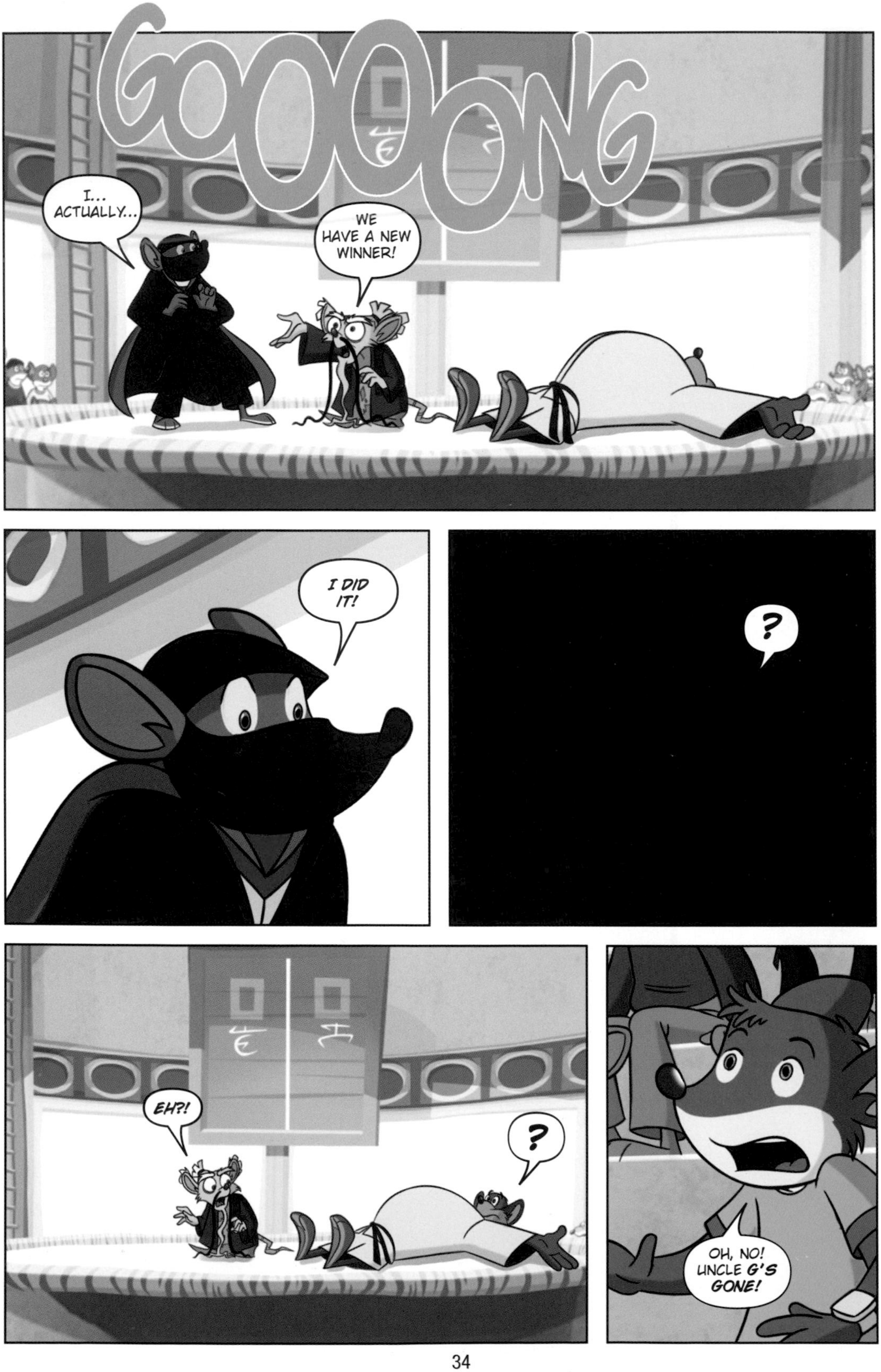
GOOOONG
I... ACTUALLY...
WE HAVE A NEW WINNER!
I DID IT!
?
EH?!
?
OH, NO! UNCLE G'S GONE!

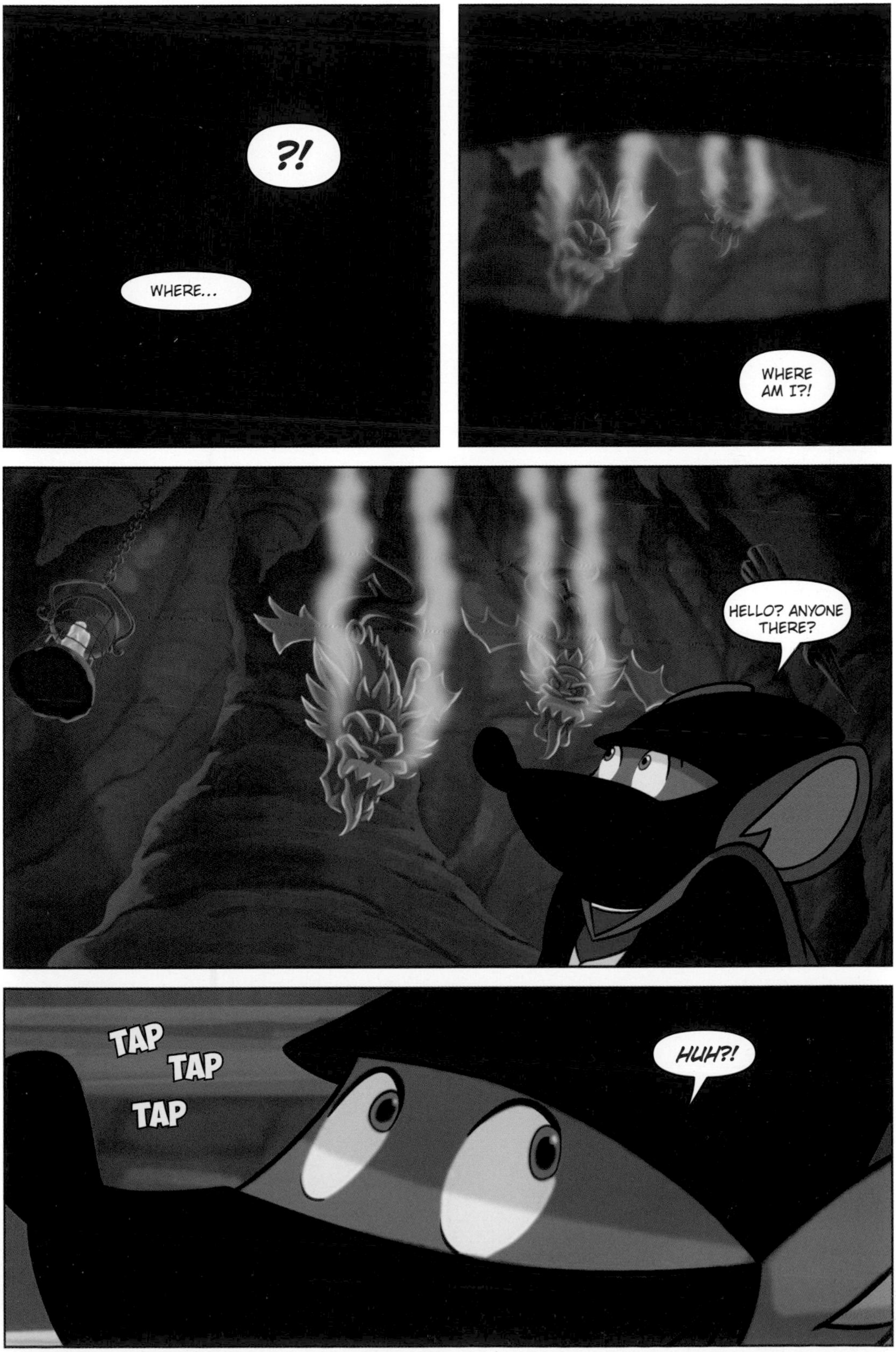
?!
WHERE...
WHERE AM I?!
HELLO? ANYONE THERE?
TAP
TAP
TAP
HUH?!

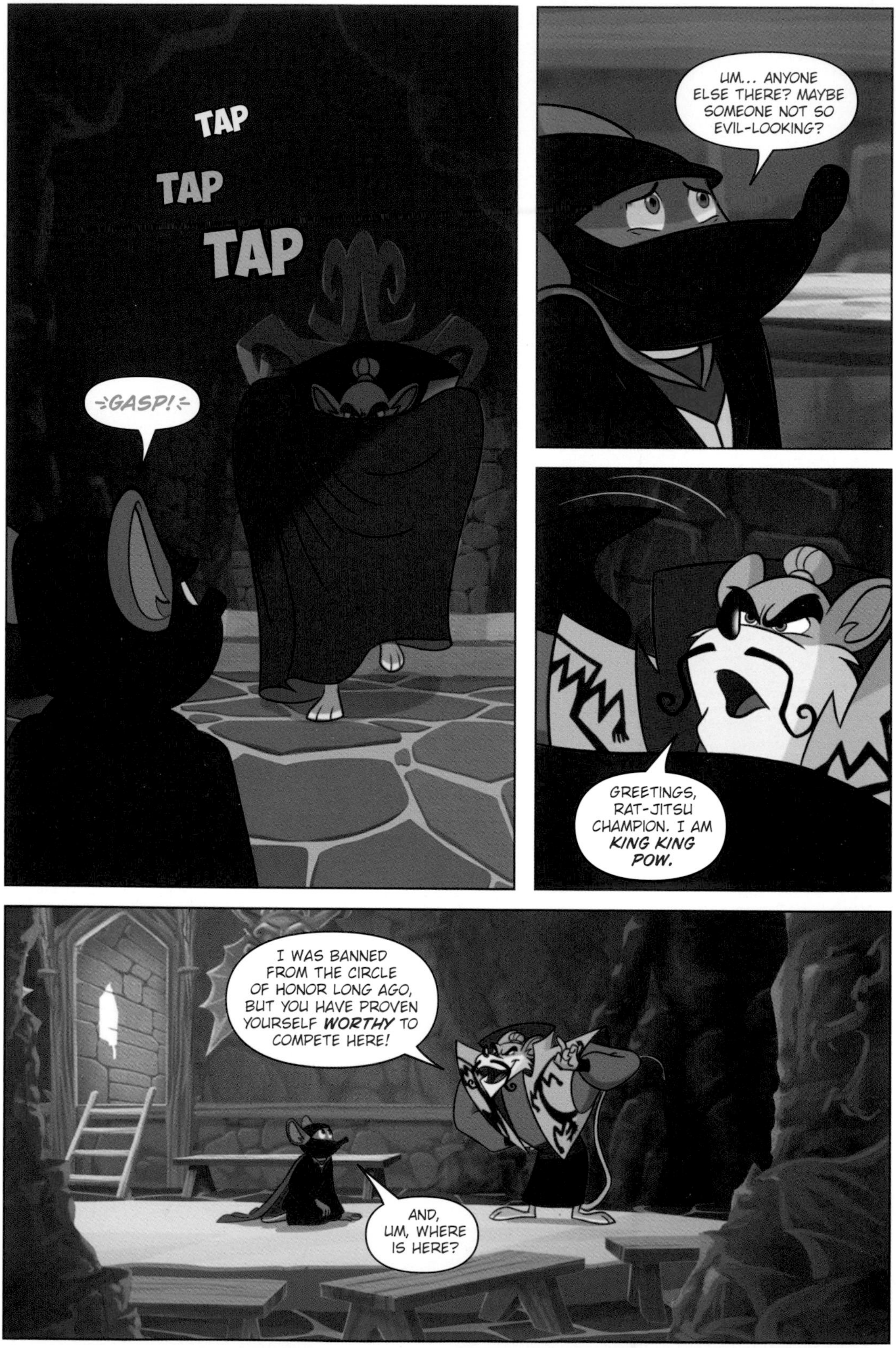
TAP
TAP
TAP
GASP!
UM... ANYONE ELSE THERE? MAYBE SOMEONE NOT SO EVIL-LOOKING?
GREETINGS, RAT-JITSU CHAMPION. I AM KING KING POW.
I WAS BANNED FROM THE CIRCLE OF HONOR LONG AGO, BUT YOU HAVE PROVEN YOURSELF WORTHY TO COMPETE HERE!
AND, UM, WHERE IS HERE?

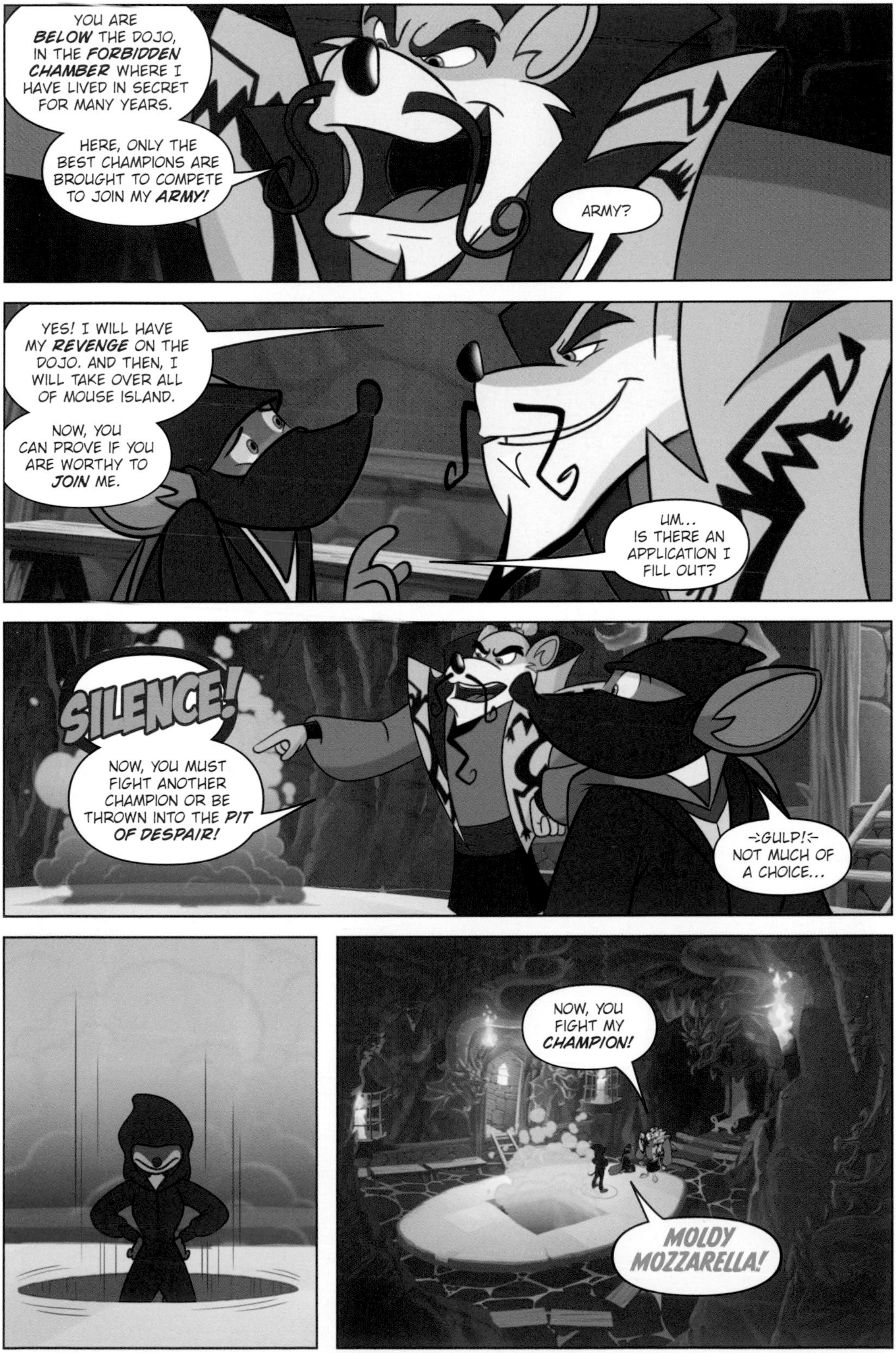

YOU ARE BELOW THE DOJO, IN THE FORBIDDEN CHAMBER WHERE I HAVE LIVED IN SECRET FOR MANY YEARS.
HERE, ONLY THE BEST CHAMPIONS ARE BROUGHT TO COMPETE TO JOIN MY ARMY!
ARMY?
YES! I WILL HAVE MY REVENGE ON THE DOJO. AND THEN, I WILL TAKE OVER ALL OF MOUSE ISLAND.
NOW, YOU CAN PROVE IF YOU ARE WORTHY TO JOIN ME.
UM... IS THERE AN APPLICATION I FILL OUT?
SILENCE!
NOW, YOU MUST FIGHT ANOTHER CHAMPION OR BE THROWN INTO THE PIT OF DESPAIR!
-GULP!- NOT MUCH OF A CHOICE...
NOW, YOU FIGHT MY CHAMPION!
MOLDY MOZZARELLA!

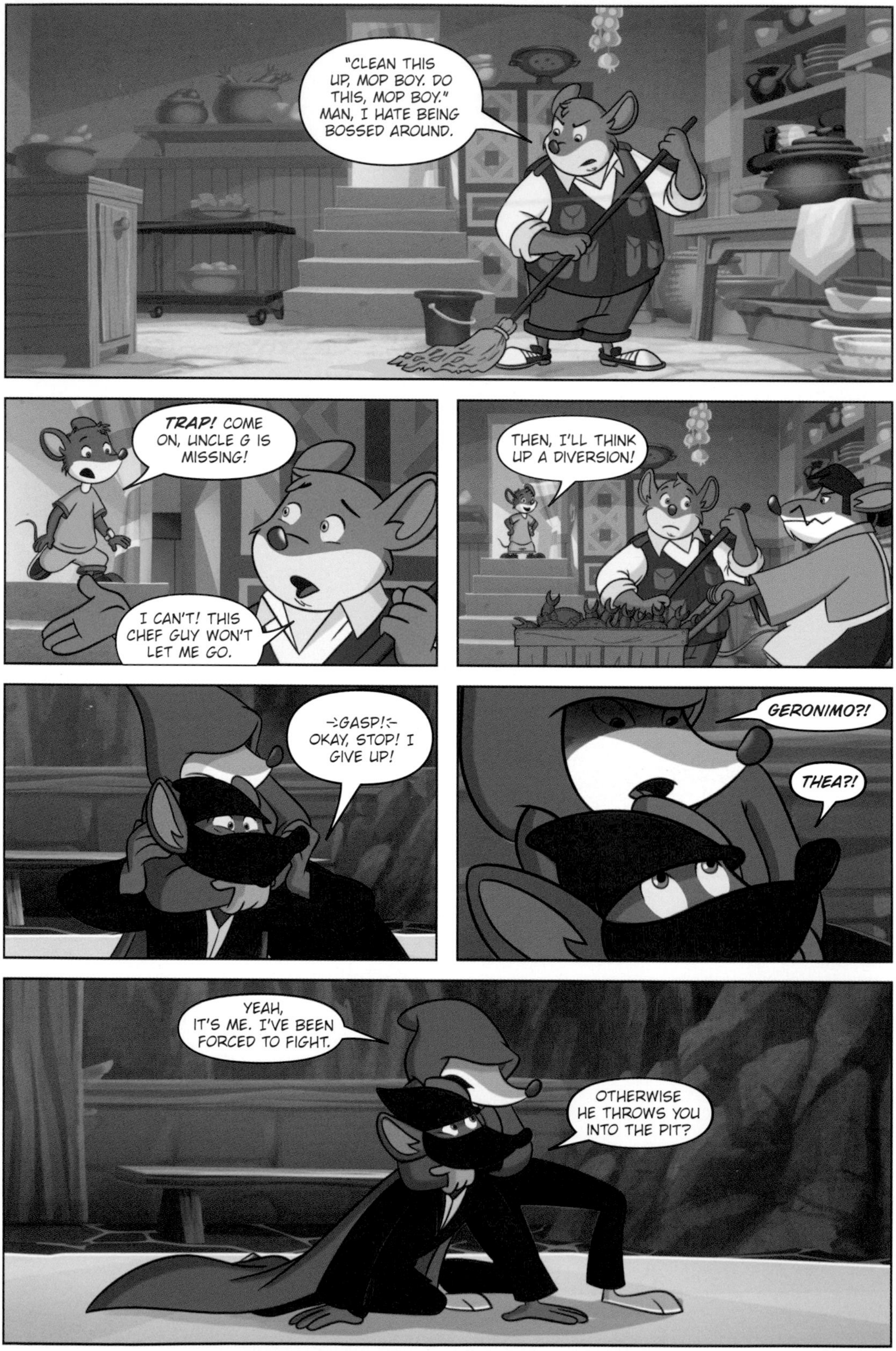
"CLEAN THIS UP, MOP BOY. DO THIS, MOP BOY." MAN, I HATE BEING BOSSED AROUND.
TRAP! COME ON, UNCLE G IS MISSING!
I CAN'T! THIS CHEF GUY WON'T LET ME GO.
THEN, I'LL THINK UP A DIVERSION!
-GASP!- OKAY, STOP! I GIVE UP!
GERONIMO?!
THEA?!
YEAH, IT'S ME. I'VE BEEN FORCED TO FIGHT.
OTHERWISE HE THROWS YOU INTO THE PIT?

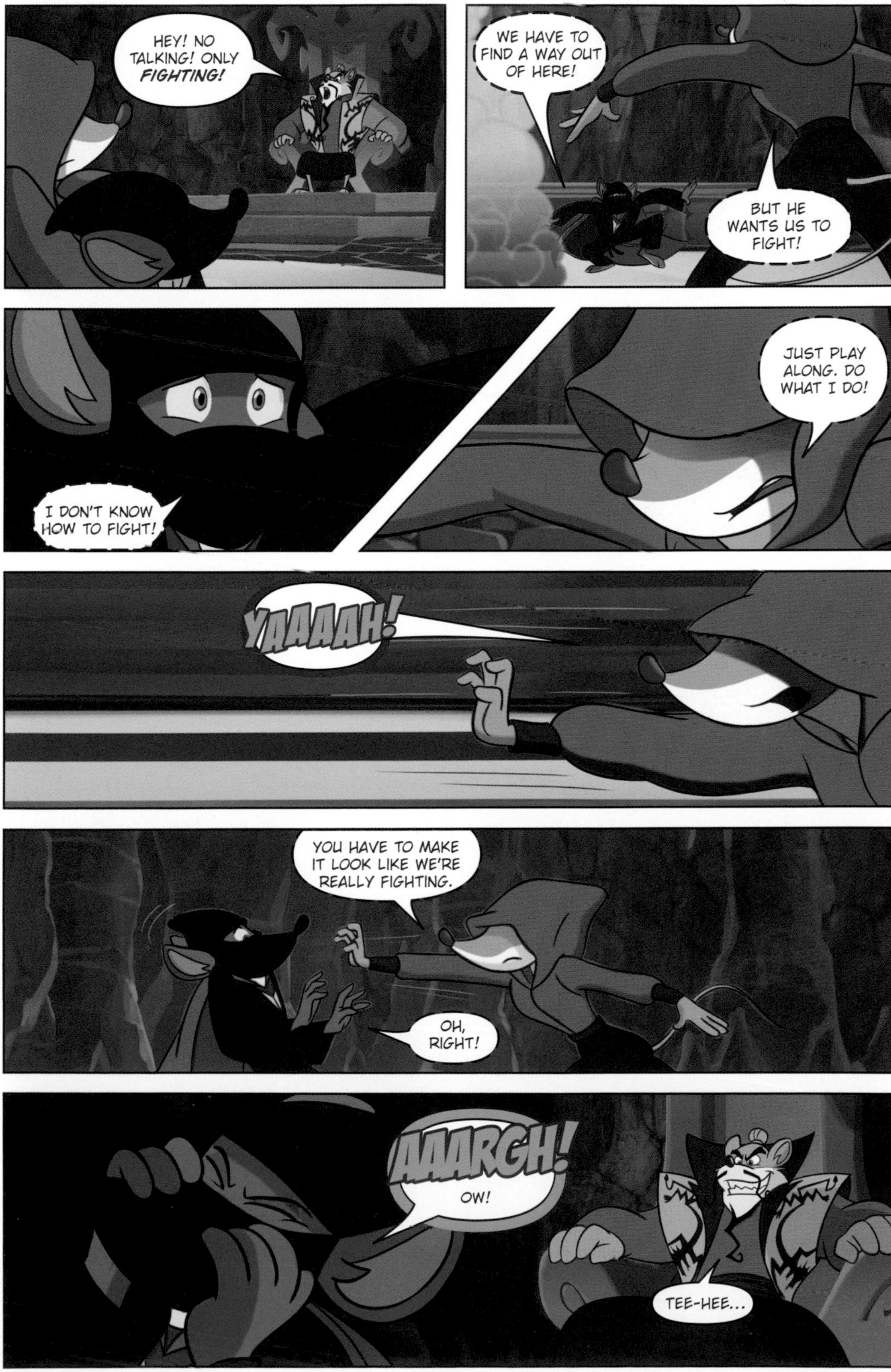
HEY! NO TALKING! ONLY FIGHTING!
WE HAVE TO FIND A WAY OUT OF HERE!
BUT HE WANTS US TO FIGHT!
I DON'T KNOW HOW TO FIGHT!
JUST PLAY ALONG. DO WHAT I DO!
YAAAAH!
YOU HAVE TO MAKE IT LOOK LIKE WE'RE REALLY FIGHTING.
OH, RIGHT!
AAARGH!
OW!
TEE-HEE...

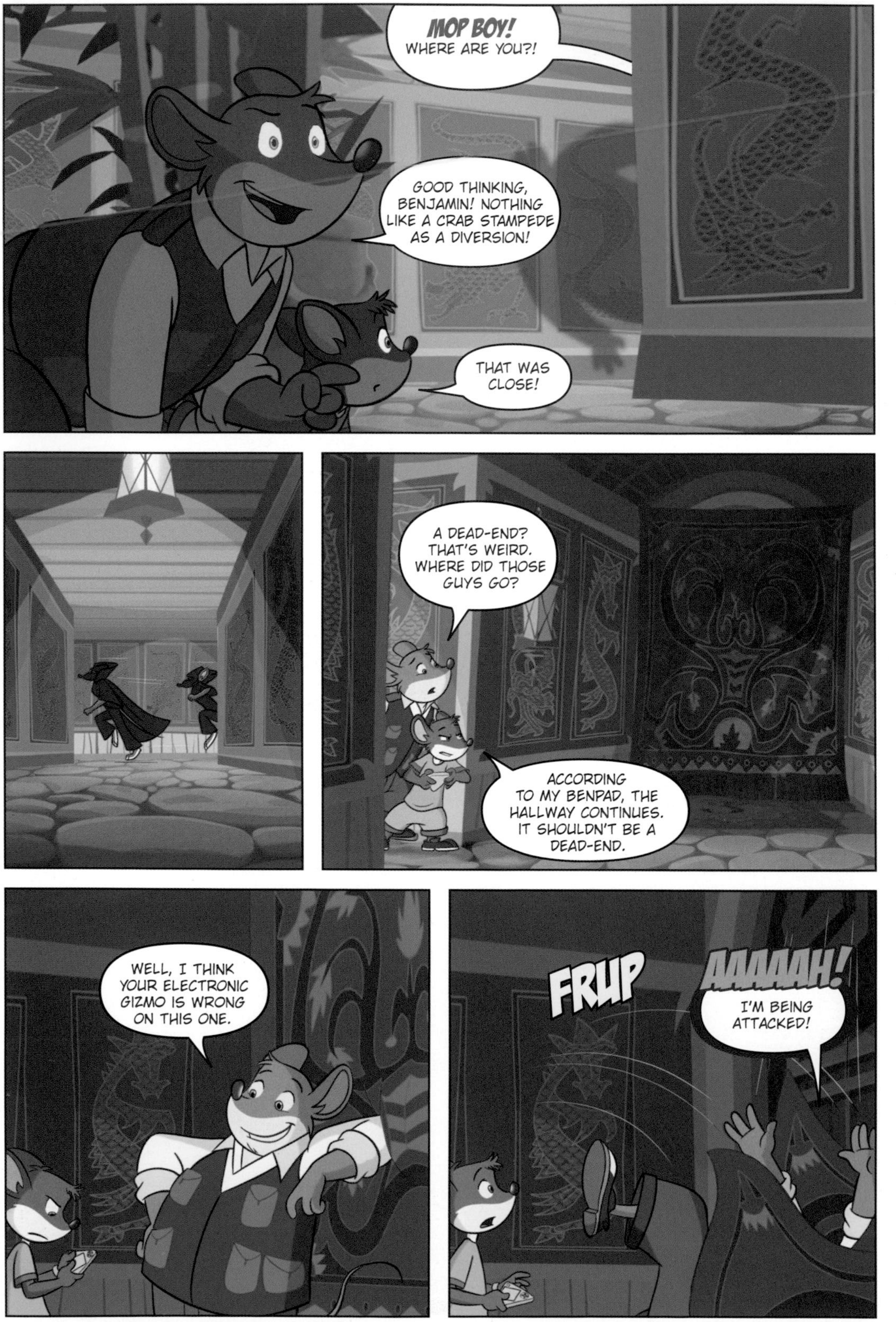

MOP BOY! WHERE ARE YOU?!
GOOD THINKING, BENJAMIN! NOTHING LIKE A CRAB STAMPEDE AS A DIVERSION!
THAT WAS CLOSE!
A DEAD-END? THAT'S WEIRD. WHERE DID THOSE GUYS GO?
ACCORDING TO MY BENPAD, THE HALLWAY CONTINUES. IT SHOULDN'T BE A DEAD-END.
WELL, I THINK YOUR ELECTRONIC GIZMO IS WRONG ON THIS ONE.
FRUP
AAAAAH! I'M BEING ATTACKED!

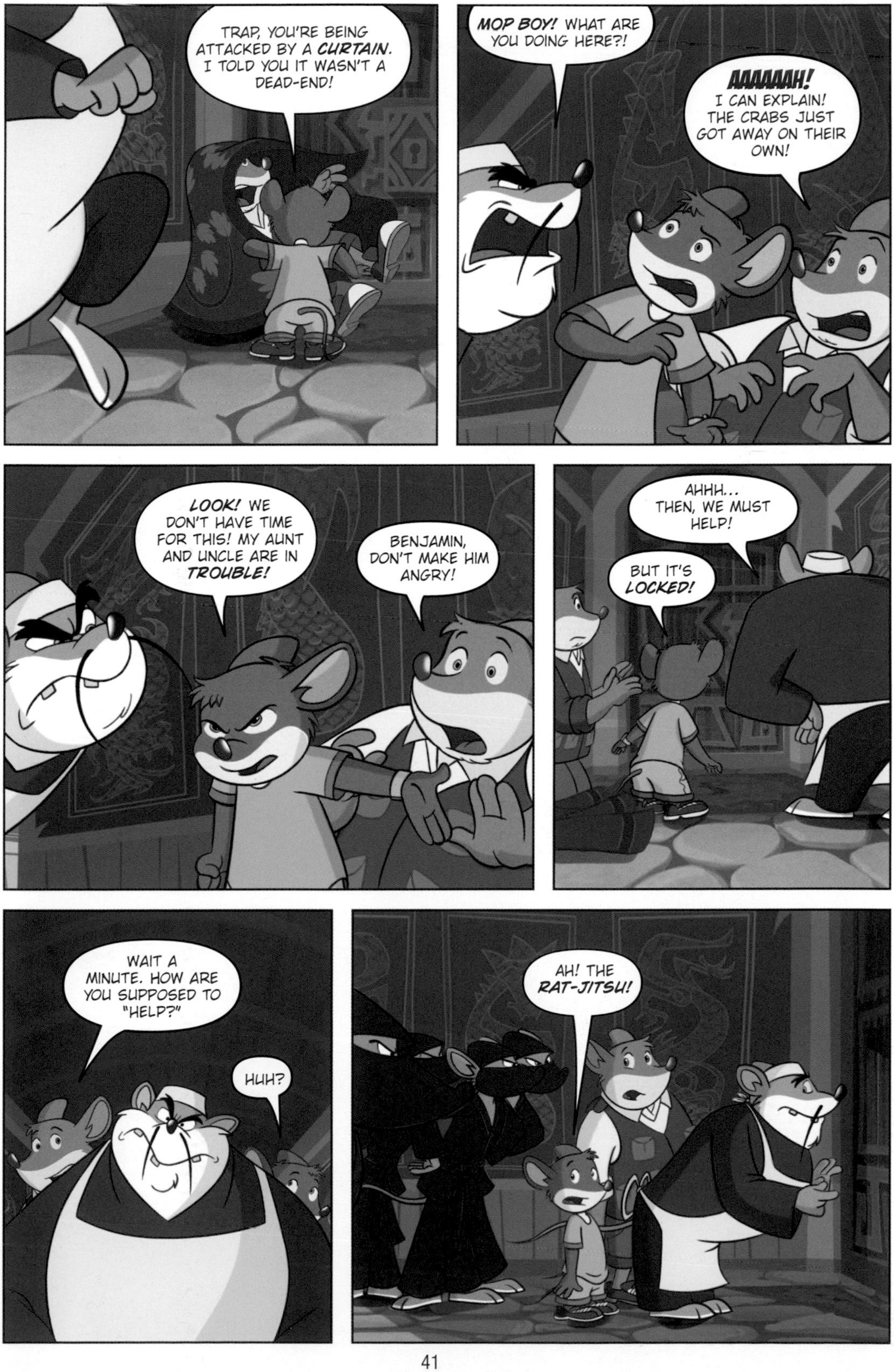
TRAP, YOU'RE BEING ATTACKED BY A CURTAIN. I TOLD YOU IT WASN'T A DEAD-END!
MOP BOY! WHAT ARE YOU DOING HERE?!
AAAAAAH! I CAN EXPLAIN! THE CRABS JUST GOT AWAY ON THEIR OWN!
LOOK! WE DON'T HAVE TIME FOR THIS! MY AUNT AND UNCLE ARE IN TROUBLE!
BENJAMIN, DON'T MAKE HIM ANGRY!
AHHH... THEN, WE MUST HELP!
BUT IT'S LOCKED!
WAIT A MINUTE. HOW ARE YOU SUPPOSED TO "HELP?"
HUH?
AH! THE RAT-JITSU!

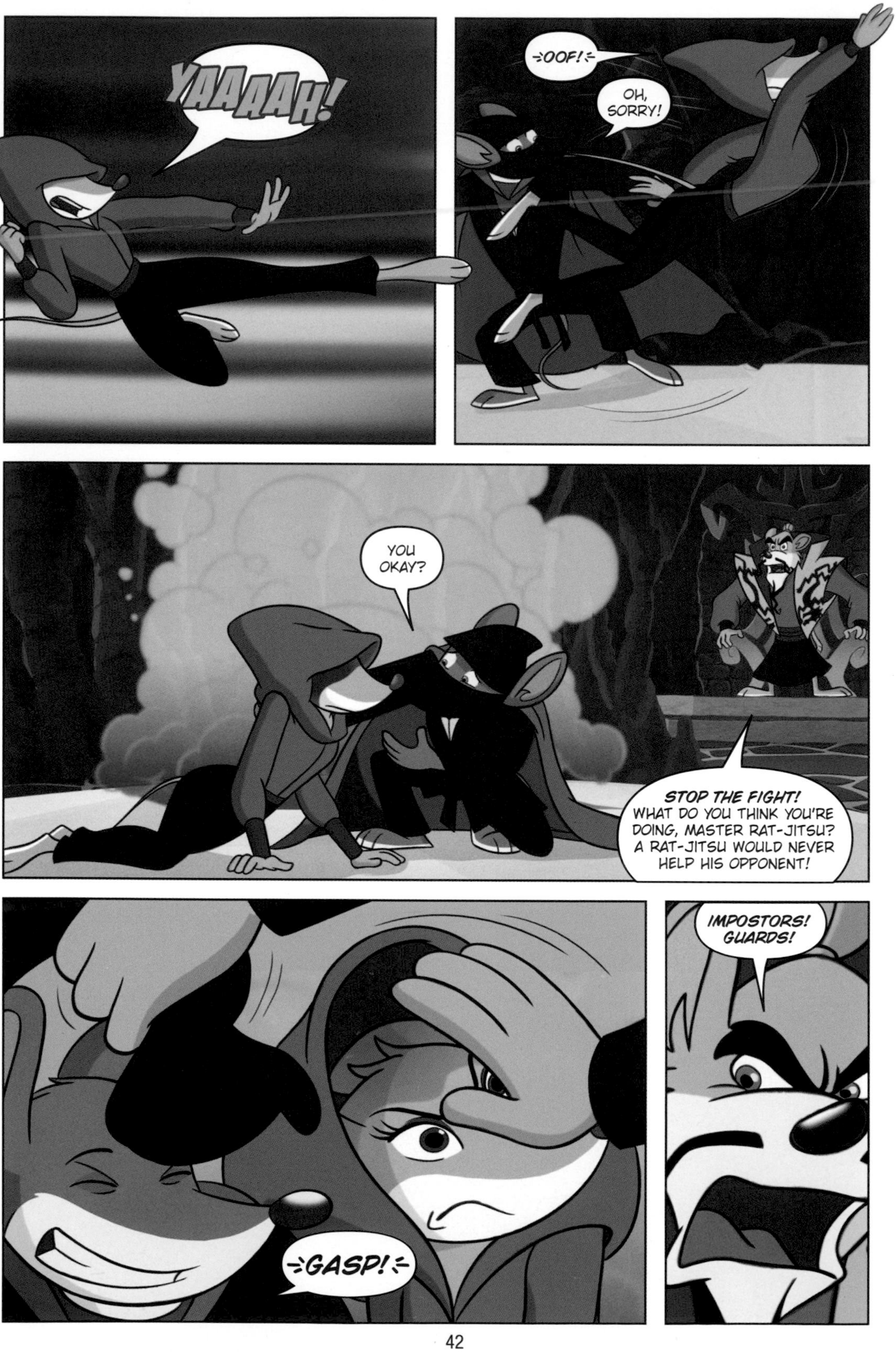
YAAAAAH!
OOF!
OH, SORRY!
YOU OKAY?
STOP THE FIGHT! WHAT DO YOU THINK YOU'RE DOING, MASTER RAT-JITSU? A RAT-JITSU WOULD NEVER HELP HIS OPPONENT!
GASP!
IMPOSTORS! GUARDS!

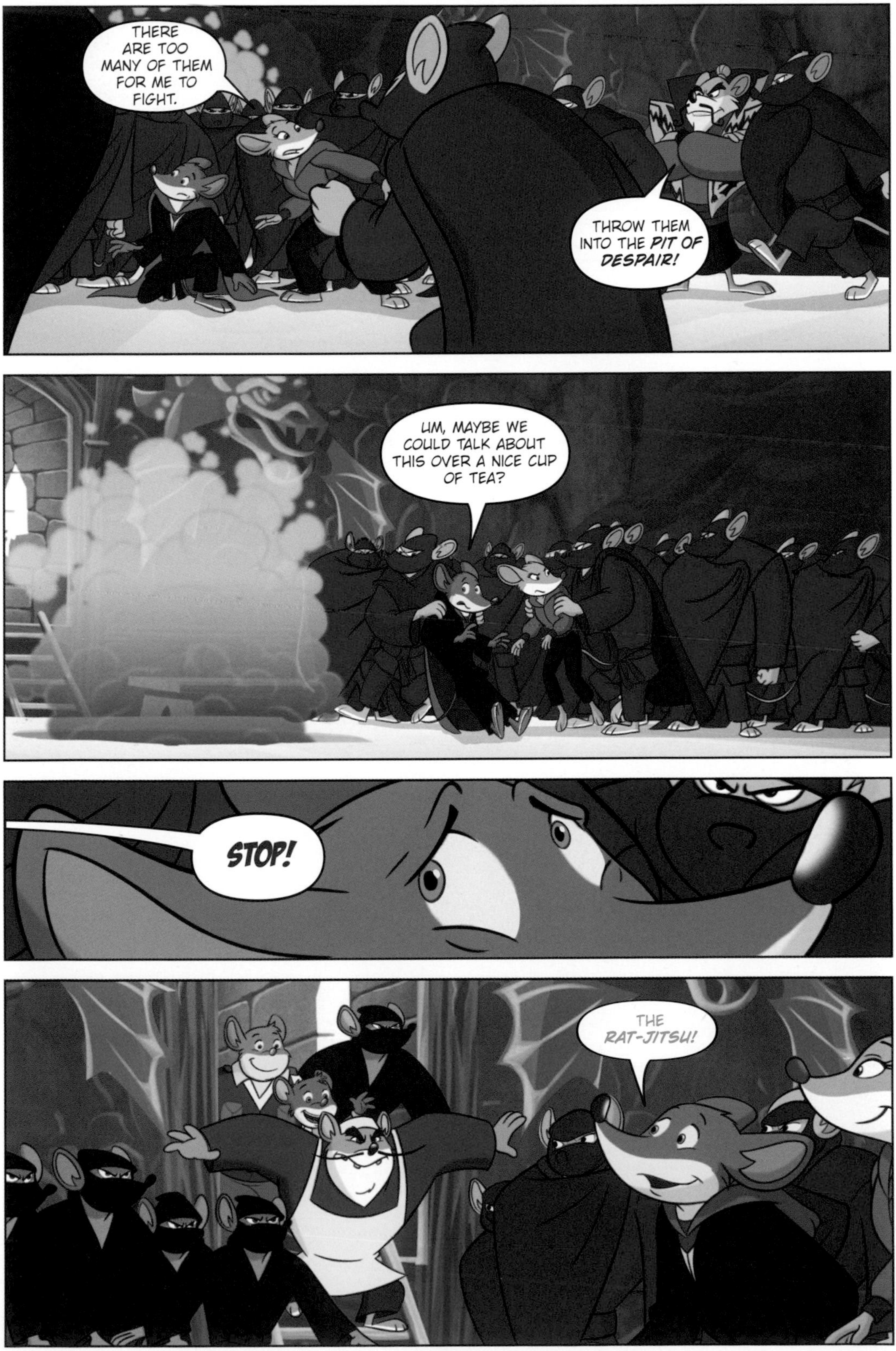
THERE ARE TOO MANY OF THEM FOR ME TO FIGHT.
THROW THEM INTO THE *PIT OF DESPAIR!*
UM, MAYBE WE COULD TALK ABOUT THIS OVER A NICE CUP OF TEA?
STOP!
THE *RAT-JITSU!*

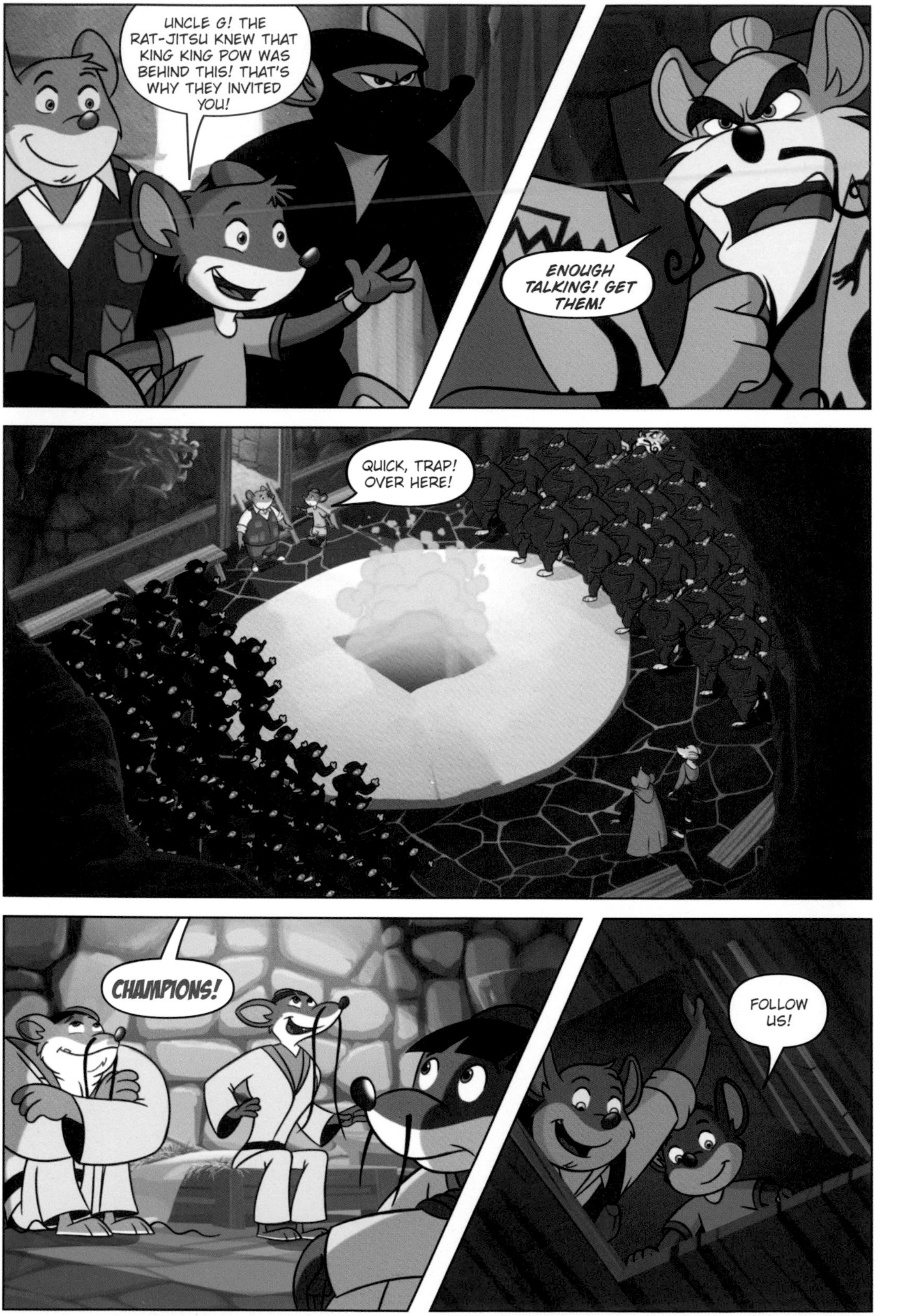
UNCLE G! THE RAT-JITSU KNEW THAT KING KING POW WAS BEHIND THIS! THAT'S WHY THEY INVITED YOU!
ENOUGH TALKING! GET THEM!
QUICK, TRAP! OVER HERE!
CHAMPIONS!
FOLLOW US!

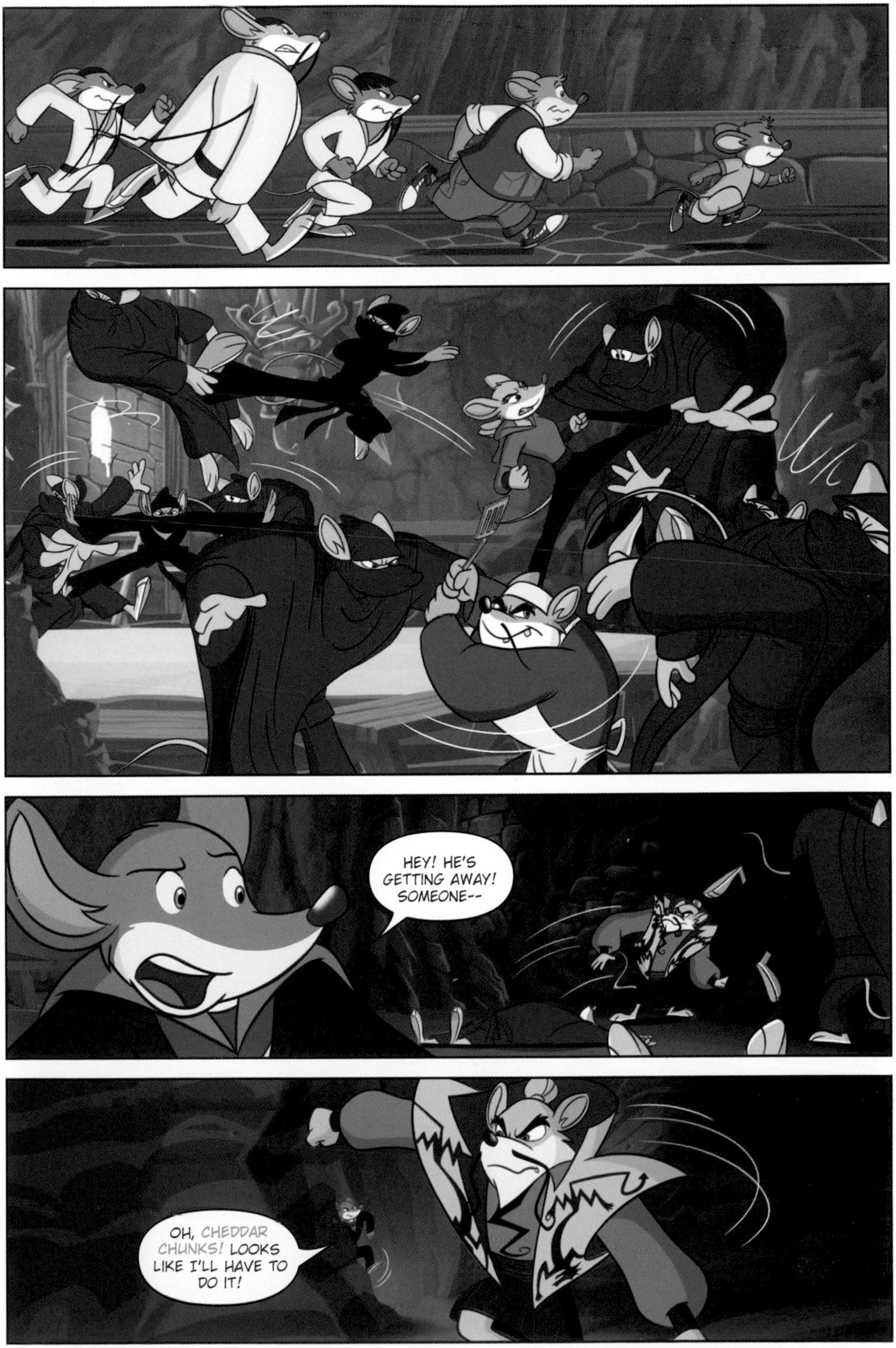
HEY! HE'S GETTING AWAY! SOMEONE--
OH, CHEDDAR CHUNKS! LOOKS LIKE I'LL HAVE TO DO IT!

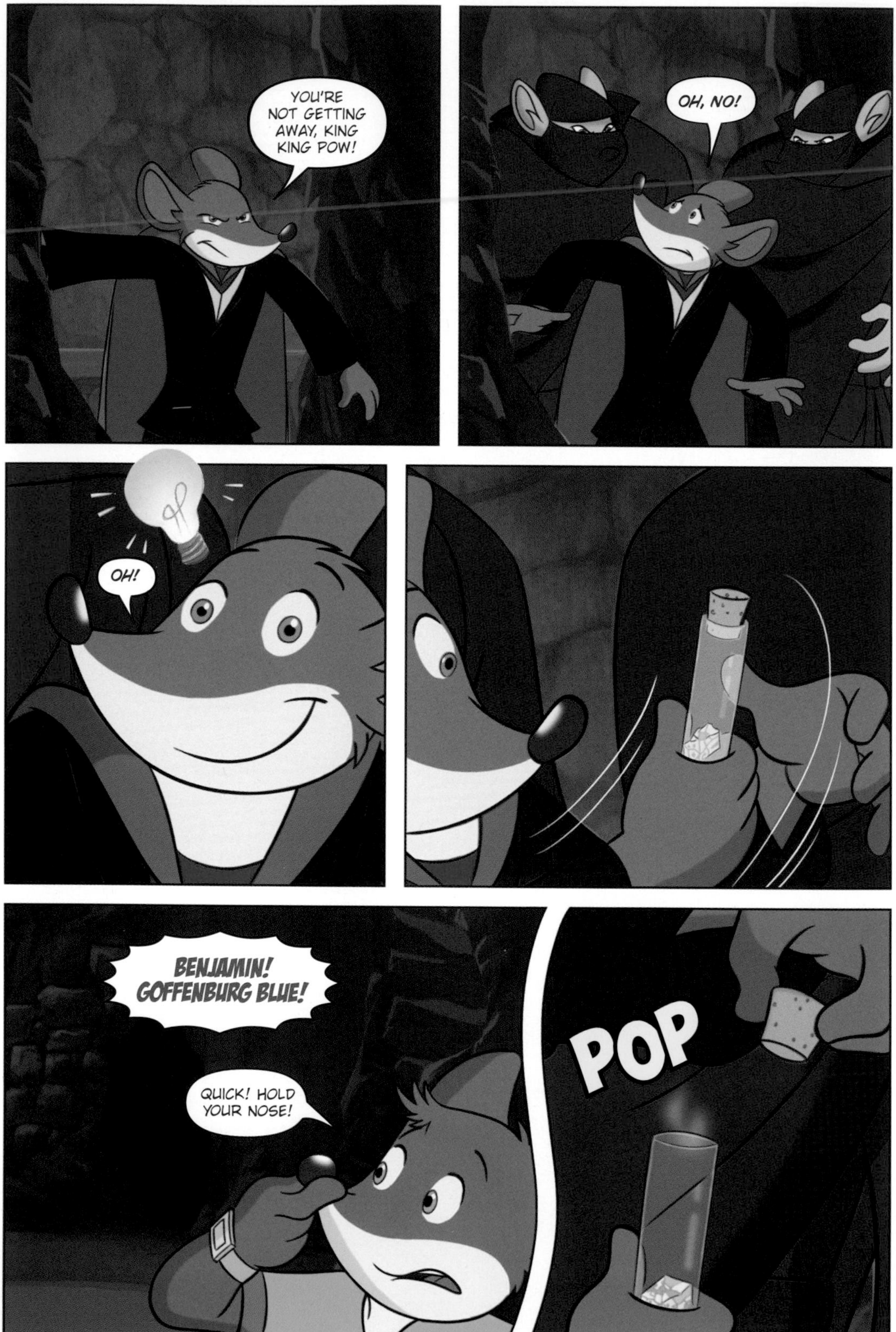

YOU'RE NOT GETTING AWAY, KING KING POW!
OH, NO!
OH!
BENJAMIN! GOFFENBURG BLUE!
QUICK! HOLD YOUR NOSE!
POP

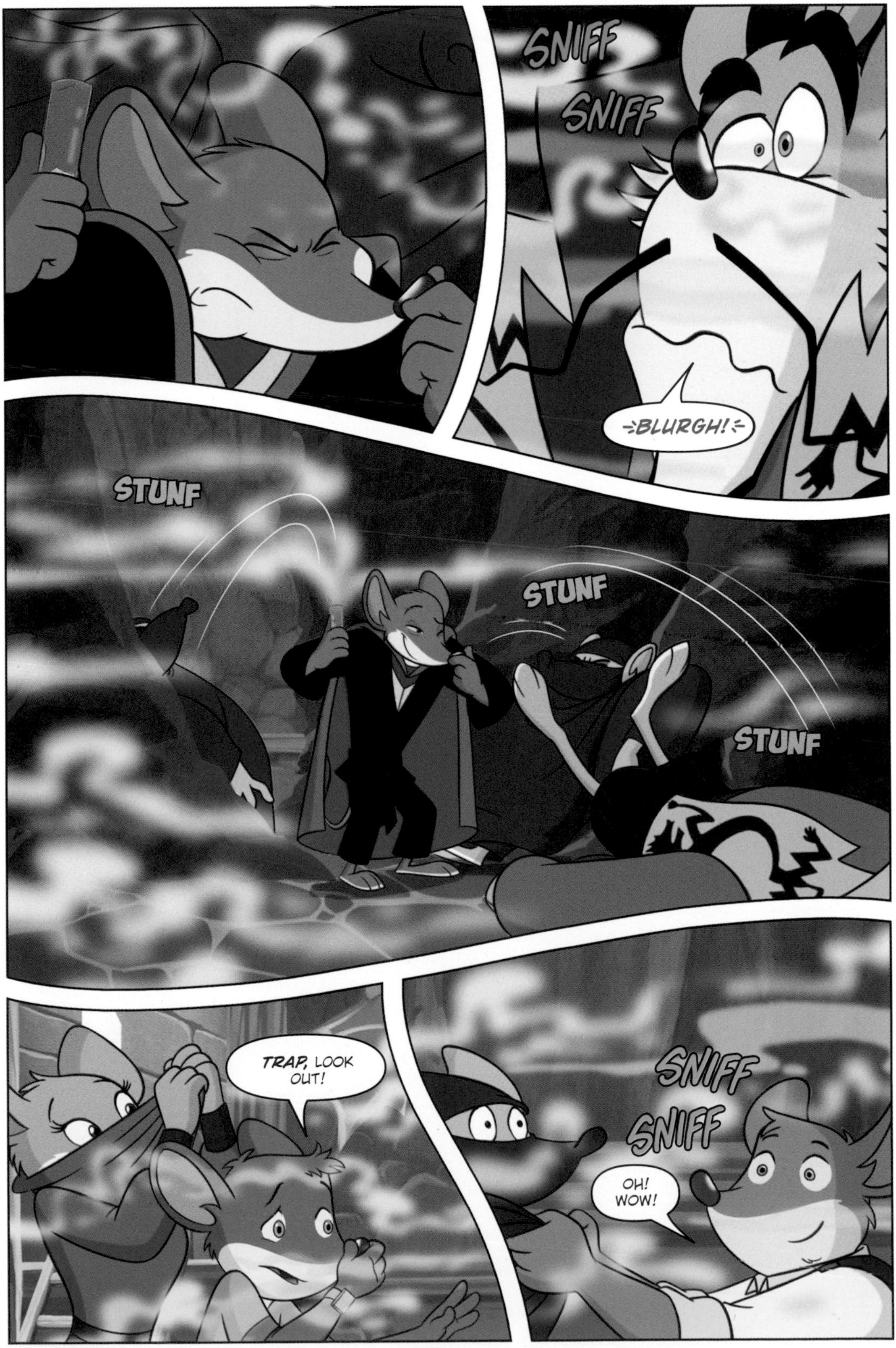
SNIFF
SNIFF
BLURGH!
STUNF
STUNF
STUNF
TRAP, LOOK OUT!
SNIFF
SNIFF
OH! WOW!

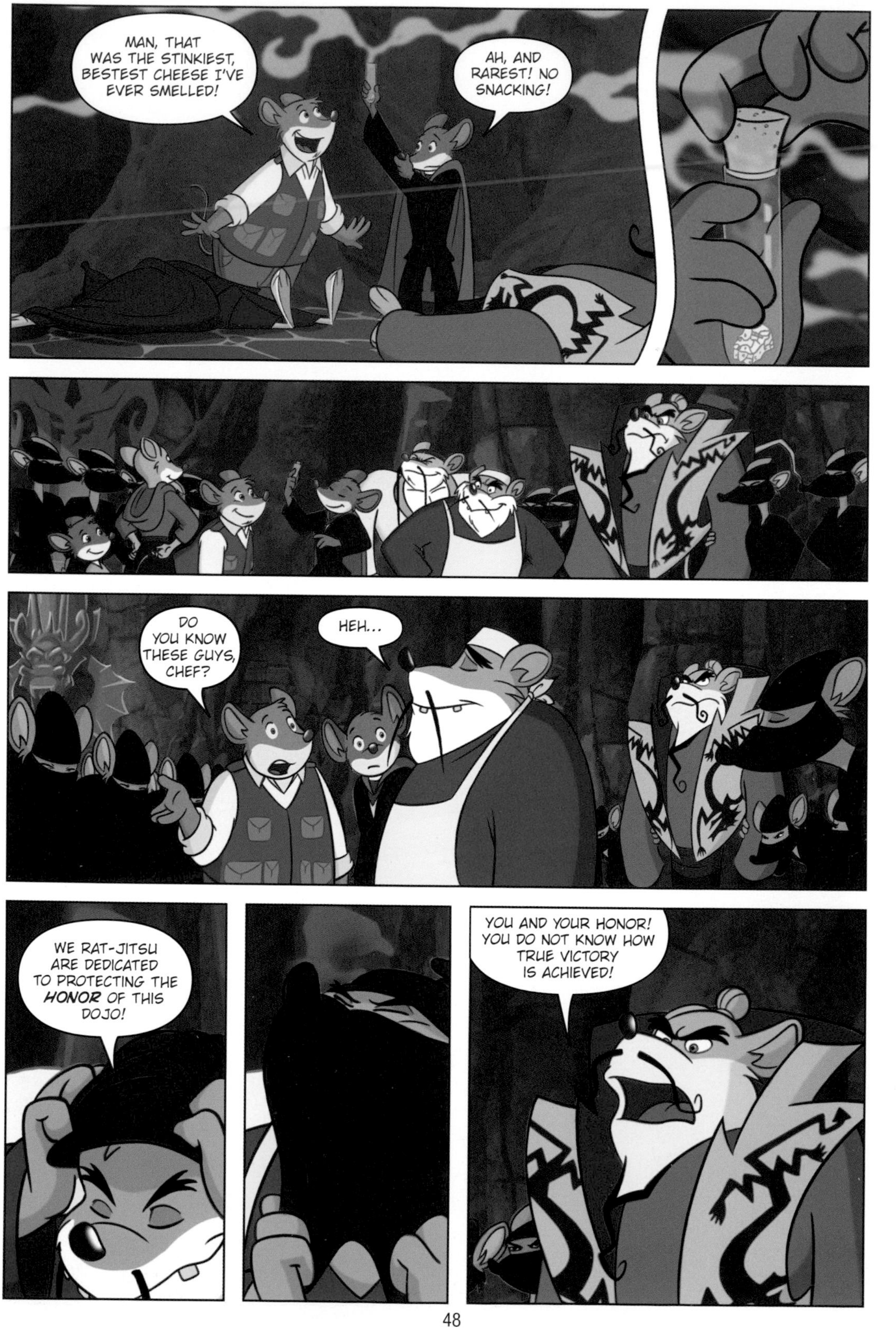
MAN, THAT WAS THE STINKIEST, BESTEST CHEESE I'VE EVER SMELLED!
AH, AND RAREST! NO SNACKING!
DO YOU KNOW THESE GUYS, CHEF?
HEH...
WE RAT-JITSU ARE DEDICATED TO PROTECTING THE HONOR OF THIS DOJO!
YOU AND YOUR HONOR! YOU DO NOT KNOW HOW TRUE VICTORY IS ACHIEVED!

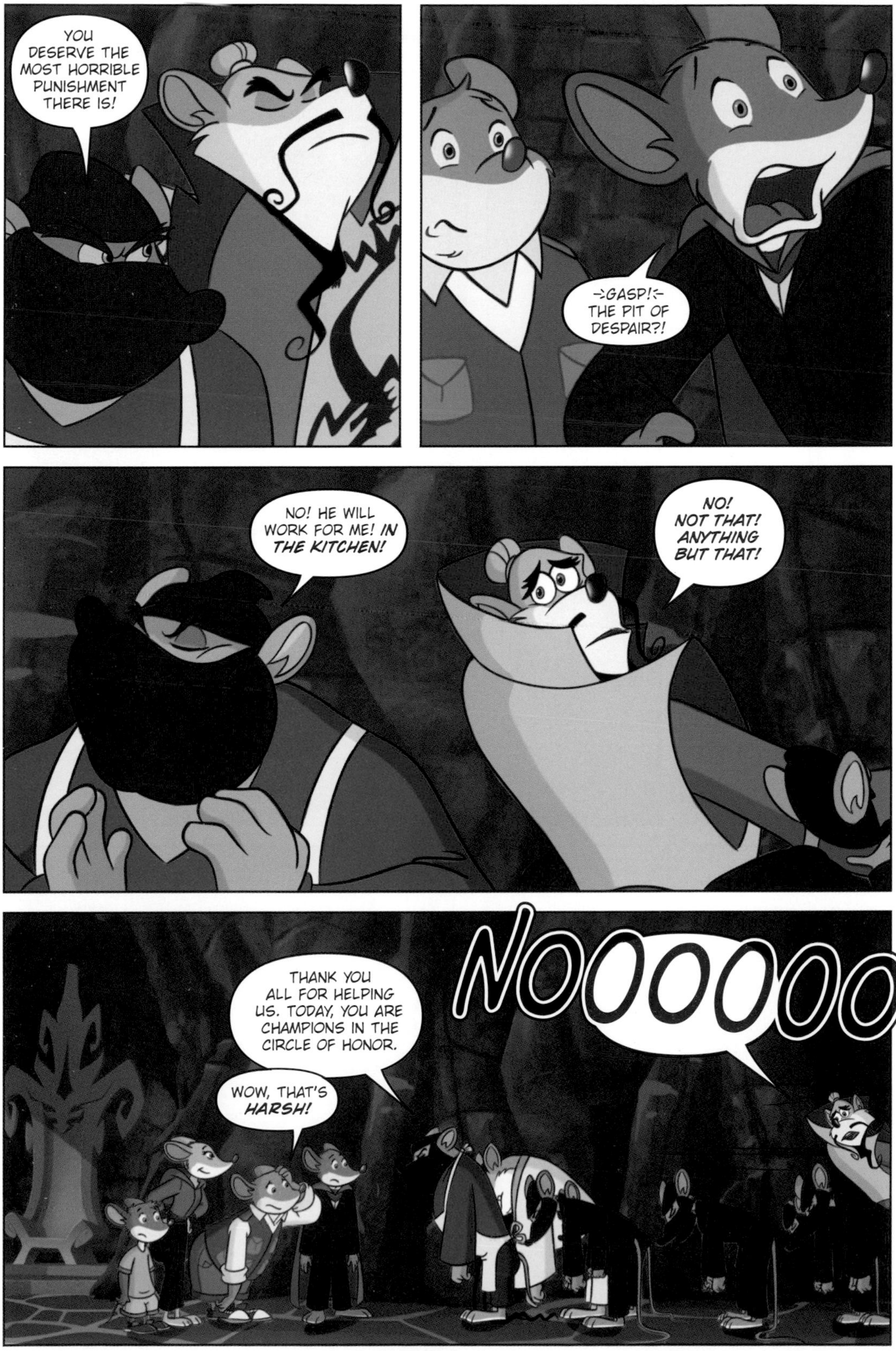
YOU DESERVE THE MOST HORRIBLE PUNISHMENT THERE IS!
-GASP!- THE PIT OF DESPAIR?!
NO! HE WILL WORK FOR ME! *IN THE KITCHEN!*
NO! NOT THAT! ANYTHING BUT THAT!
THANK YOU ALL FOR HELPING US. TODAY, YOU ARE CHAMPIONS IN THE CIRCLE OF HONOR.
WOW, THAT'S ***HARSH!***
NOOOOOO

Special Preview of GERONIMO STILTON REPORTER Graphic Novel #10
"Blackrat's Treasure"!

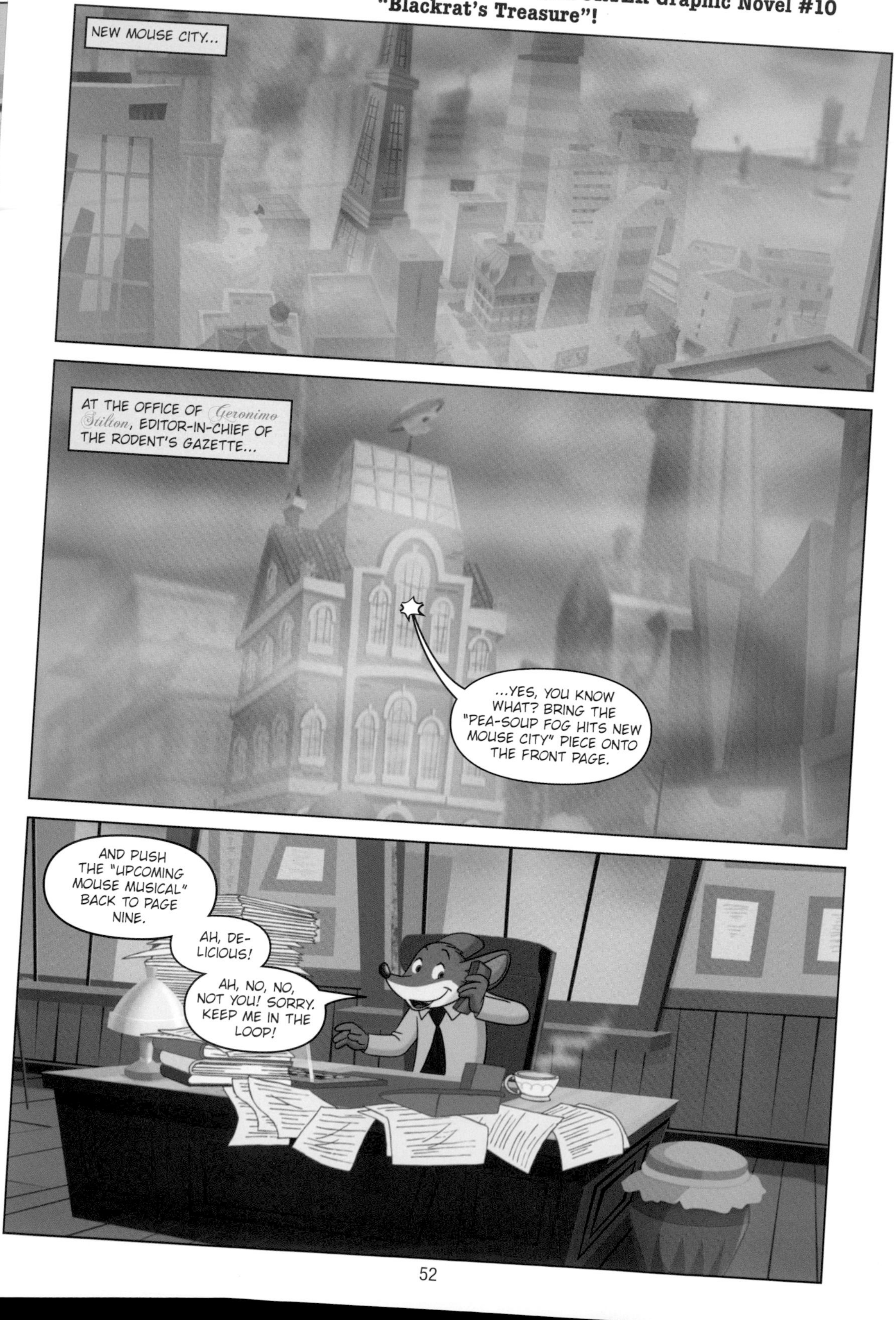
NEW MOUSE CITY...
AT THE OFFICE OF Geronimo Stilton, EDITOR-IN-CHIEF OF THE RODENT'S GAZETTE...
...YES, YOU KNOW WHAT? BRING THE "PEA-SOUP FOG HITS NEW MOUSE CITY" PIECE ONTO THE FRONT PAGE.
AND PUSH THE "UPCOMING MOUSE MUSICAL" BACK TO PAGE NINE.
AH, DE-LICIOUS!
AH, NO, NO, NOT YOU! SORRY. KEEP ME IN THE LOOP!

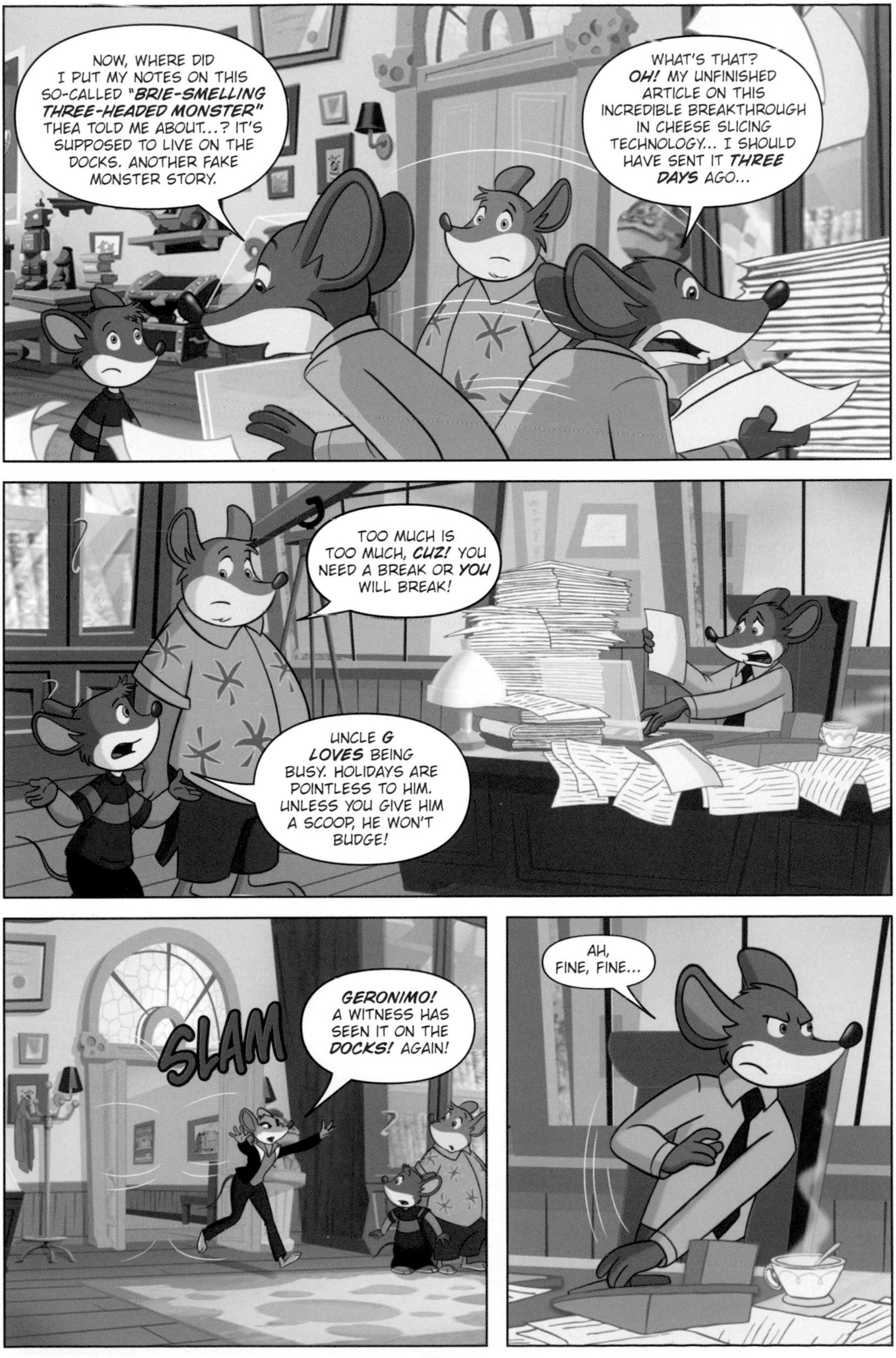

NOW, WHERE DID I PUT MY NOTES ON THIS SO-CALLED "BRIE-SMELLING THREE-HEADED MONSTER" THEA TOLD ME ABOUT...? IT'S SUPPOSED TO LIVE ON THE DOCKS. ANOTHER FAKE MONSTER STORY.
WHAT'S THAT? OH! MY UNFINISHED ARTICLE ON THIS INCREDIBLE BREAKTHROUGH IN CHEESE SLICING TECHNOLOGY... I SHOULD HAVE SENT IT THREE DAYS AGO...
TOO MUCH IS TOO MUCH, CUZ! YOU NEED A BREAK OR YOU WILL BREAK!
UNCLE G LOVES BEING BUSY. HOLIDAYS ARE POINTLESS TO HIM. UNLESS YOU GIVE HIM A SCOOP, HE WON'T BUDGE!
SLAM
GERONIMO! A WITNESS HAS SEEN IT ON THE DOCKS! AGAIN!
AH, FINE, FINE...

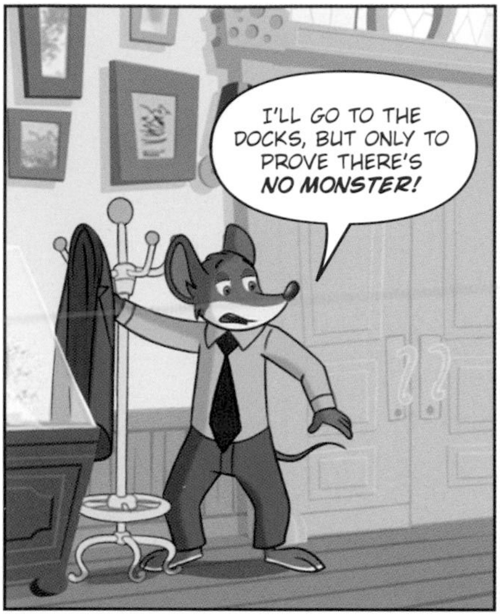
I'LL GO TO THE DOCKS, BUT ONLY TO PROVE THERE'S **NO MONSTER!**

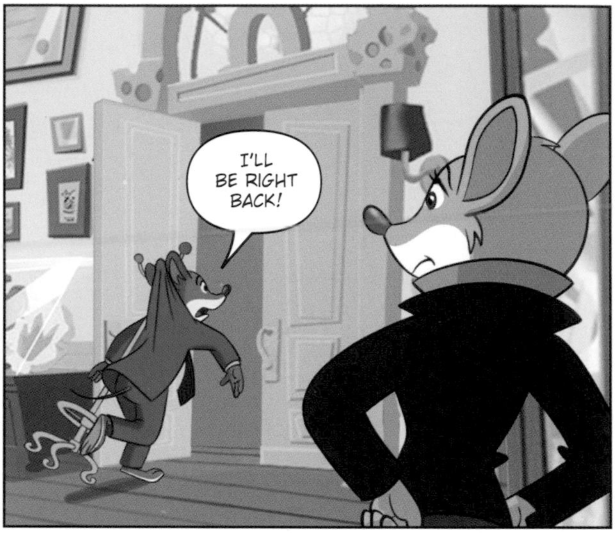
I'LL BE RIGHT BACK!

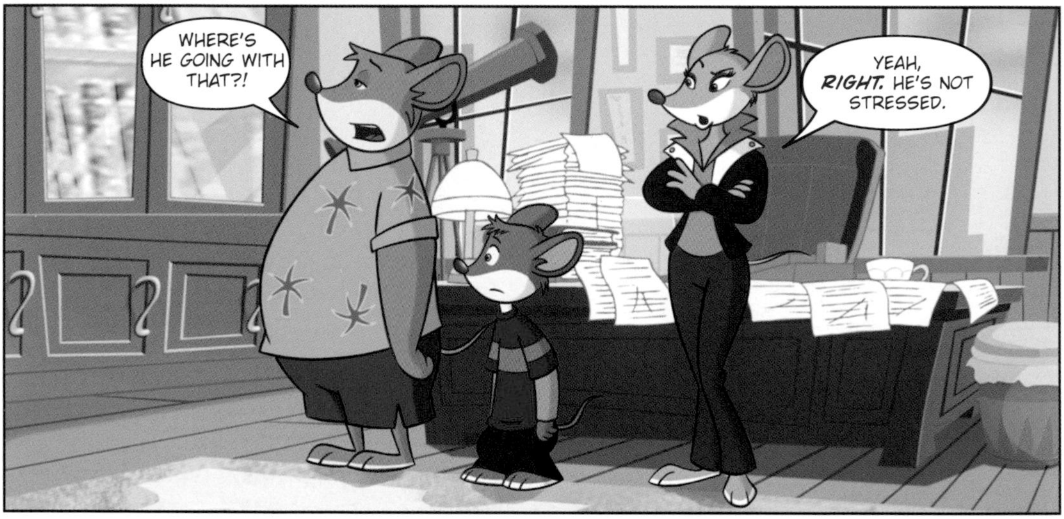
WHERE'S HE GOING WITH THAT?!
YEAH, **RIGHT.** HE'S NOT STRESSED.

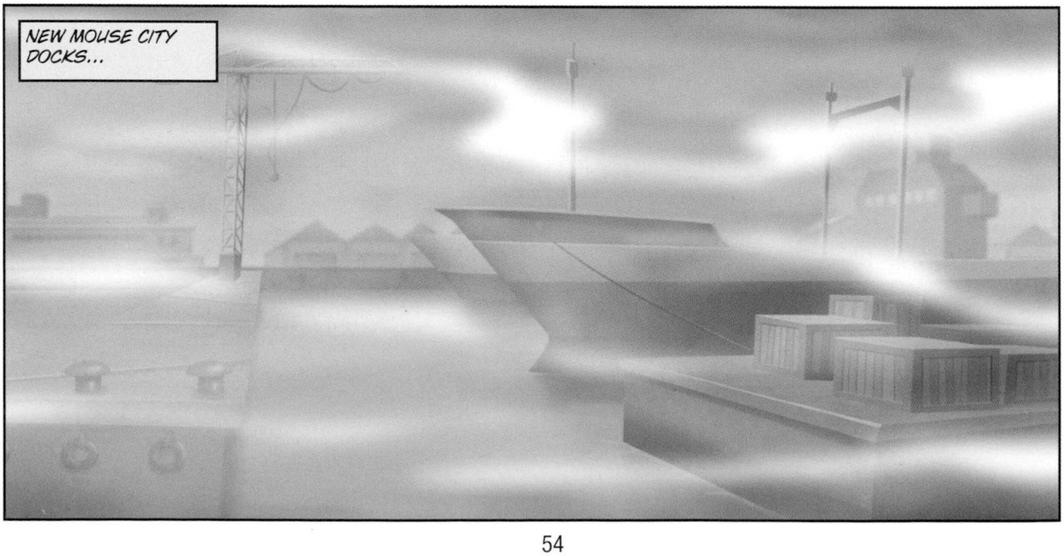
NEW MOUSE CITY DOCKS...

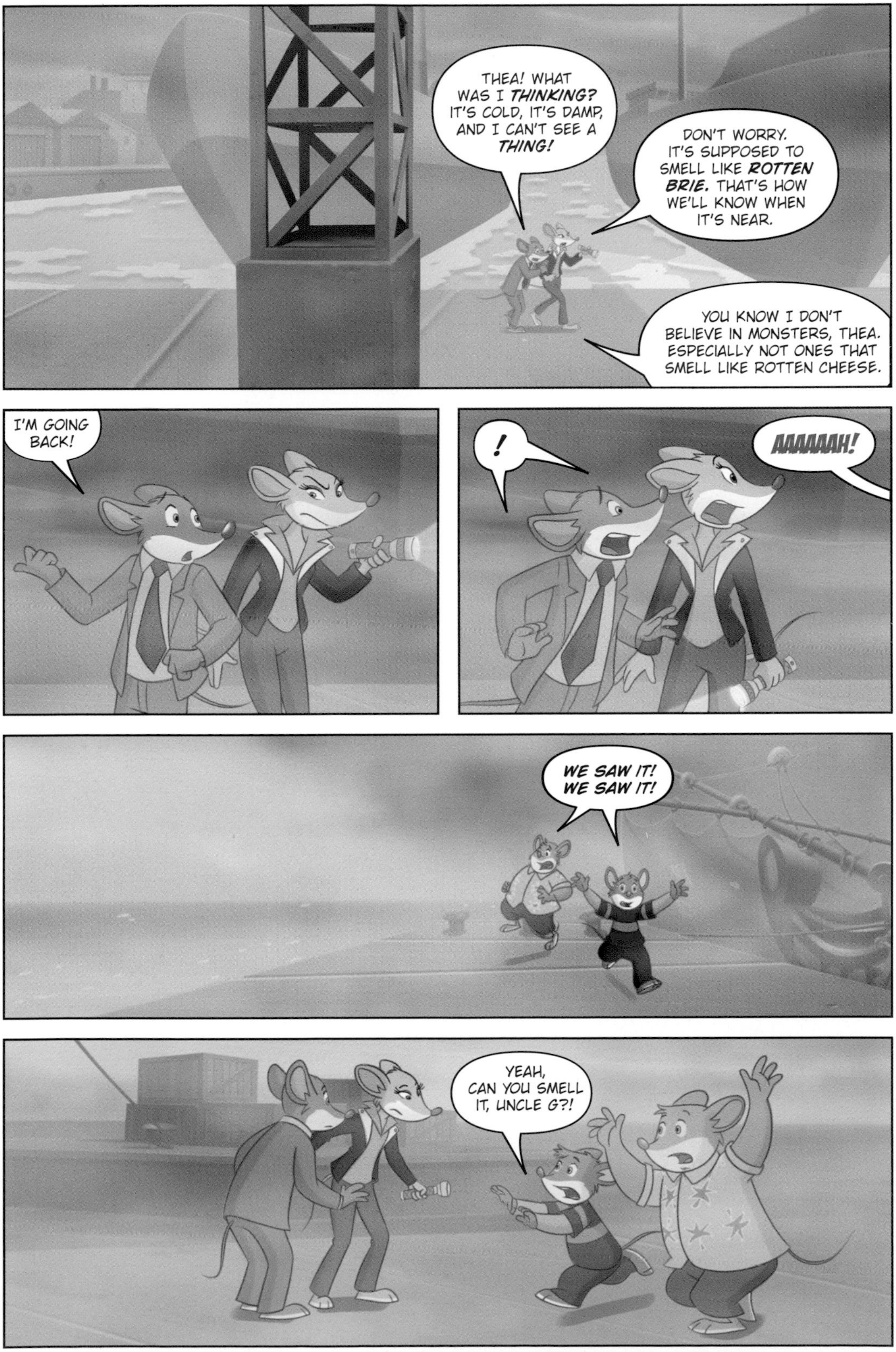

THEA! WHAT WAS I THINKING? IT'S COLD, IT'S DAMP, AND I CAN'T SEE A THING!
DON'T WORRY. IT'S SUPPOSED TO SMELL LIKE ROTTEN BRIE. THAT'S HOW WE'LL KNOW WHEN IT'S NEAR.
YOU KNOW I DON'T BELIEVE IN MONSTERS, THEA. ESPECIALLY NOT ONES THAT SMELL LIKE ROTTEN CHEESE.
I'M GOING BACK!
!
AAAAAAH!
WE SAW IT! WE SAW IT!
YEAH, CAN YOU SMELL IT, UNCLE G?!

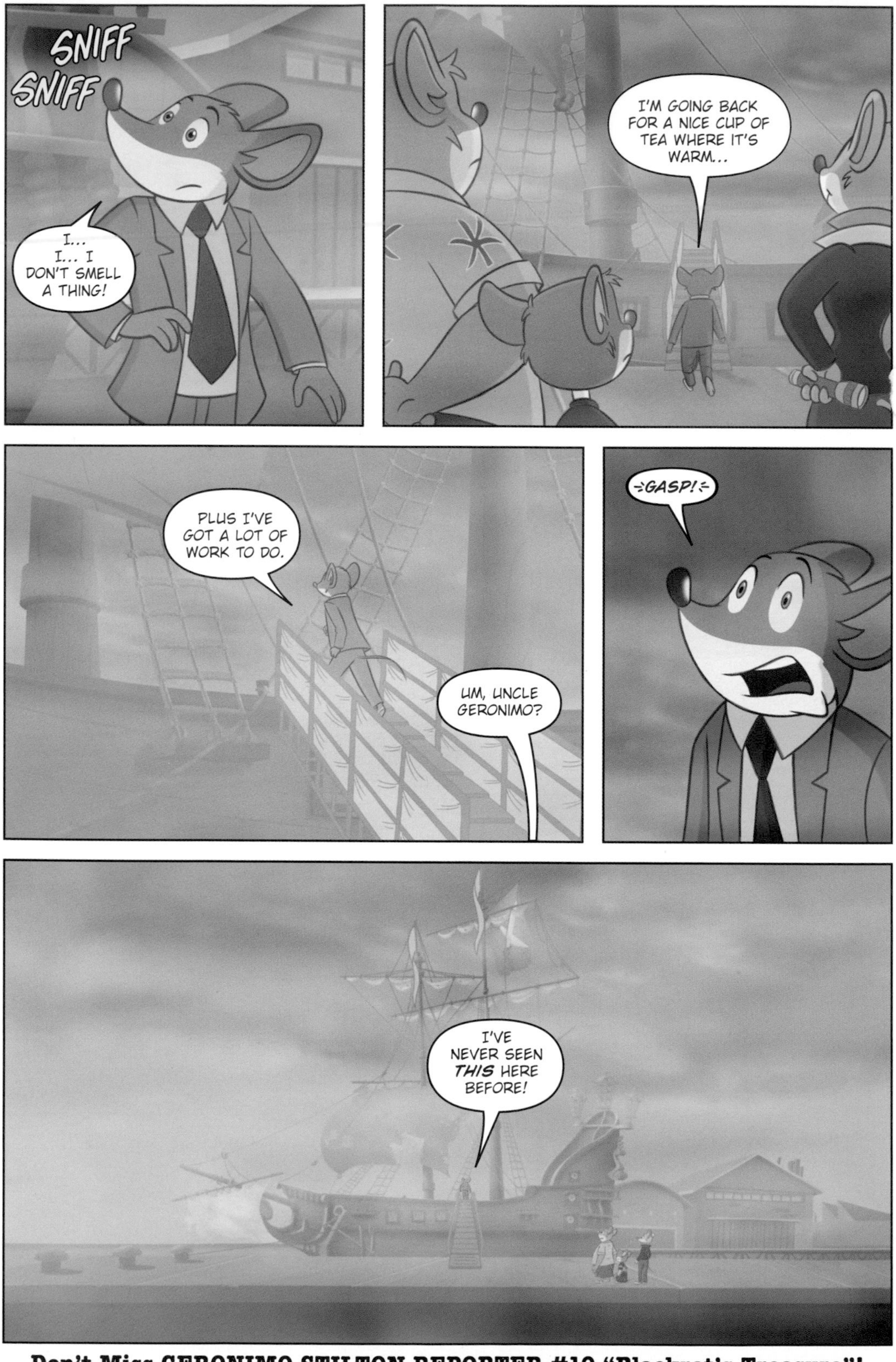
SNIFF SNIFF
I... I... I DON'T SMELL A THING!
I'M GOING BACK FOR A NICE CUP OF TEA WHERE IT'S WARM...
PLUS I'VE GOT A LOT OF WORK TO DO.
UM, UNCLE GERONIMO?
GASP!
I'VE NEVER SEEN *THIS* HERE BEFORE!

Don't Miss GERONIMO STILTON REPORTER #10 "Blackrat's Treasure"!
Coming soon!

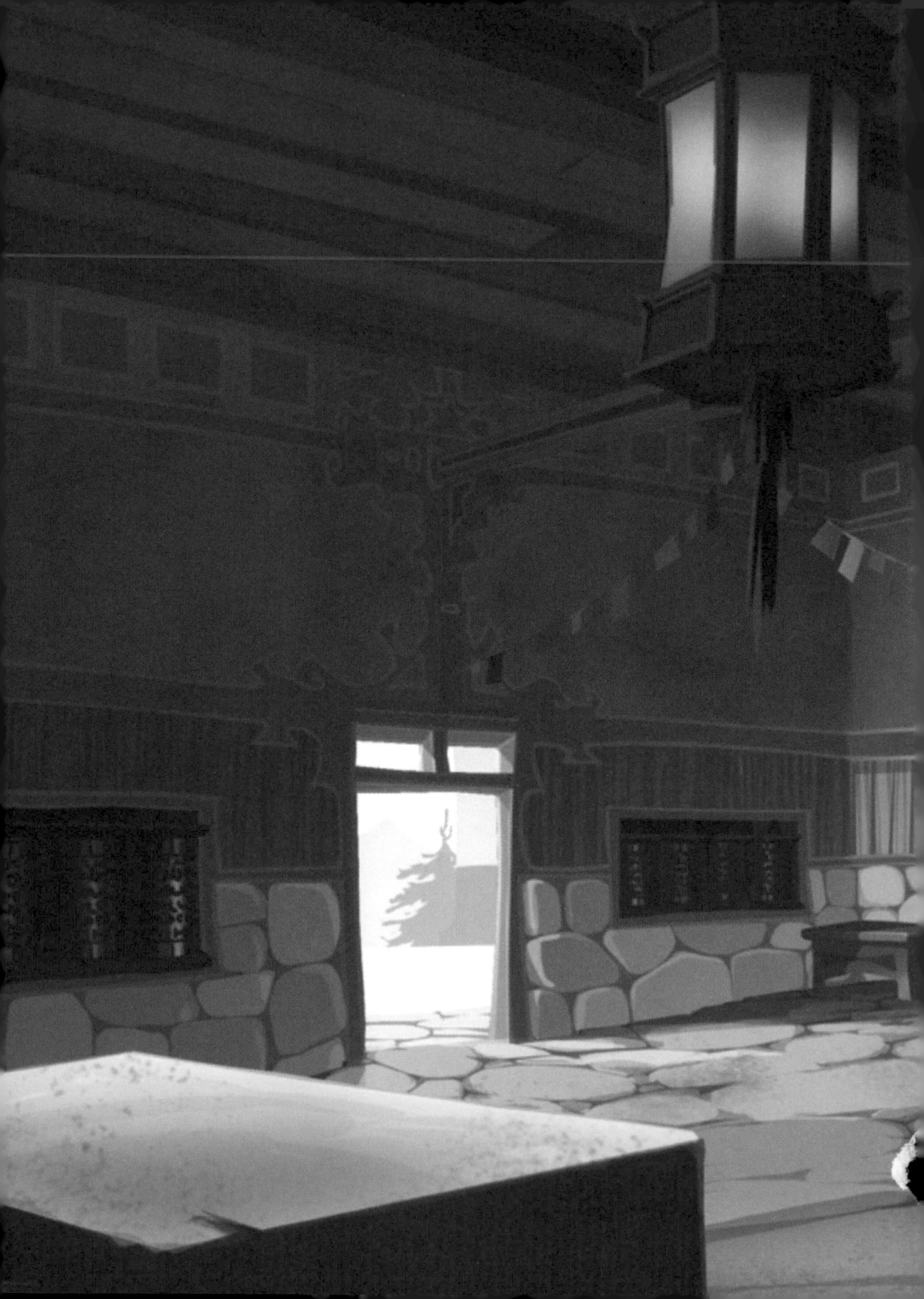